FANCY

LINDA BRODAY

FANCY

Edited by: Alyssa Howson - lyssahowson@startmail.com

Published by Epitaph Press
5814 98th St #307
Lubbock, Texas 79424

http://lindabroday.com

Version 2022.01

45,908 words.

ISBN: 978-1-7323199-3-6

CONTENTS

FANCY

LOVE TRAIN SERIES
BOOK 10

Linda Broday

ALSO BY LINDA BRODAY

Lone Star Legends:

A COWBOY OF LEGEND

A COWBOY CHRISTMAS LEGEND

A MAN OF LEGEND

Outlaw Mail Order Brides:

THE OUTLAW'S MAIL ORDER BRIDE

SAVING THE MAIL ORDER BRIDE

THE MAIL ORDER BRIDE'S SECRET

ONCE UPON A MAIL ORDER BRIDE

Men of Legend Series:

TO LOVE A TEXAS RANGER

HEART OF A TEXAS COWBOY

TO MARRY A TEXAS OUTLAW

The Bachelors of Battle Creek Series:

TEXAS MAIL ORDER BRIDE

TWICE A TEXAS BRIDE

FOREVER HIS TEXAS BRIDE

Texas Heroes:

KNIGHT ON THE TEXAS PLAINS

THE COWBOY WHO CAME CALLING

TO CATCH A TEXAS STAR

Single Title:

FANCY (Love Train Series) August 2022

TEXAS REDEMPTION

Anthologies:

THE COWBOY WHO SAVED CHRISTMAS

LONGING FOR A COWBOY CHRISTMAS

GUNSMOKE AND LACE

CHRISTMAS IN A COWBOY'S ARMS

GIVE ME A TEXAN

GIVE ME A COWBOY

GIVE ME A TEXAS RANGER

GIVE ME A TEXAS OUTLAW

A TEXAS CHRISTMAS

BE MY TEXAS VALENTINE

HEARTS AND SPURS

Dear Reader,

I was thrilled when I got a chance to join the multi-author Love Train series authors and take part in this exciting project. I love trains and love the places it can take us. Fancy's story came to me almost right away and I embarked on a journey with her. Her story was heartbreaking, and I made a vow to myself to give her a happy ending, although I had no idea how I was going to do that at the outset. But if you've read one of my books, you know I always promise a happy ending.

In real life we're beset with good times and bad like a rollercoaster with ups, downs, hairpin curves, and periods of smooth sailing—and we navigate everything at dangerous speeds. As Fancy Dalton boards the Union Pacific #1216 and sets off on this harrowing journey to find her stolen baby, she doesn't know if she'll succeed or fail. There are no guarantees. She only knows she'll risk everything—even her life—to find her baby son and get him back.

This train has a bit of magical power, uniting couples and sparking love. I think that's due to the matchmaking conductor, Henry Manners. A very lovely man with a heart of gold.

Fancy need not feel she's embarked on this journey alone. Help comes in the form of Jack Coltrain, a rugged cowboy on his own mission. He's exactly the kind of man she needs. Jack is strong, mentally and physically, and possesses enormous determination in putting Fancy's baby back in her empty arms.

As with all good stories, this journey isn't without peril. Danger gets Fancy's and Jack's hearts beating faster and makes them more tenacious. I hope you like the twists and turns I've strewn into the path. I can't have you getting bored. Now, can I?

So, sit back and enjoy this new adventure. I'm dipping my toes in the self-publishing waters and I think I may like it. I have a sweet historical western romance series that will be coming before too long so subscribe to my newsletter so you won't miss it.

Enjoy and celebrate each one of Fancy's and Jack's triumphs and setbacks.

Until next time,

Linda Broday

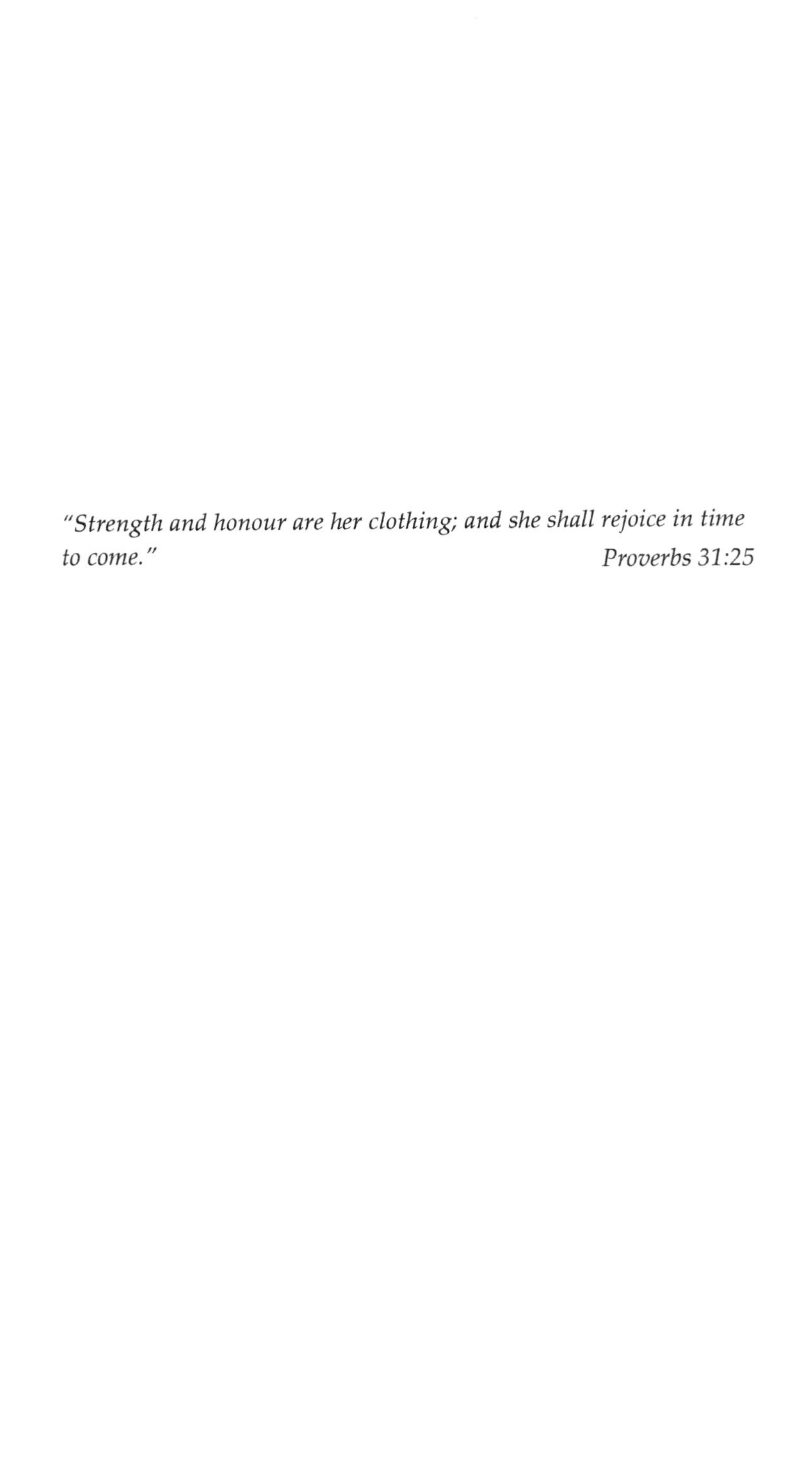

"Strength and honour are her clothing; and she shall rejoice in time to come." *Proverbs 31:25*

PROLOGUE

Saratoga, Nebraska
1879

Her baby was coming! There was nothing she could do to stop it.

Searing pains stole her breath as Fancy Dalton collapsed in a heap on the Saratoga, Nebraska street, warm water gushing from her. She clutched her stomach, looking desperately at the passersby, scanning for a friendly face. If she couldn't get to the midwife several blocks away, she'd have her child in the dirt.

With a loud cry, she bent double, sweat breaking out on her forehead.

"Please, someone help me," she cried.

A woman in a dove gray dress and white apron suddenly stooped over her. She appeared to quickly access the situation. "Ma'am, I'm Mrs. Judith Winters, a midwife."

"I have to get to Grant Street," Fancy gasped. "Hurry."

Mrs. Winters wiped beads of sweat from Fancy's forehead.

"I doubt we have time, dear. I live two doors down. I'll take care of you. I've done this a few hundred times." She helped Fancy stand. "Please, take my arm."

The woman had kind hazel eyes and a gentle voice. An angel.

Yes, the answer to a prayer.

"Thank you so much for your kindness, Mrs. Winters."

Fancy leaned heavily on her and they moved slowly toward a nearby door. She might have a chance.

"What is your name, dear?" Mrs. Winters asked.

"Fancy…Fancy Dalton. Bless you for helping." She managed a weak smile.

Once they began moving, she felt in less dire straits. Then out of the blue, the severe pains hit again, and she went down to her knees. "The baby's coming. I can feel it."

The midwife lifted her up. "Take some panting breaths, dear. We're almost there." The woman opened a door. "Here we are." She led her to a bed and spread a thick piece of oilcloth over the sheet to protect it. "We'll get you into a gown then you can lie down."

A woman's loud sobs erupted from another part of the house. "Do you need to see about that poor soul, Mrs. Winters?"

"Her husband is consoling her. Please tell me a little about yourself." The woman helped her undress.

"My mother and I live near where we work." Fancy doubled over again and released a cry. When the pains passed, she went on. "I work at the Whistle Stop Café. My mother washes clothes in Henry King's Laundry. It's not too far. Will you please go fetch her? Please?" Fancy gasped out the words. "I need her."

"I will in a bit. We have things to do here, and I don't think there's time. Get into bed." Mrs. Winters no sooner spread a sheet over her than Fancy clutched her stomach and cried out in agony.

"Please help me," Fancy begged, tears running down her cheeks. "The pain..."

"I need to check you." The midwife pressed around on Fancy's swollen stomach. "You'll have your baby in no time. So you have no husband?"

"No. This is the result of an—attack—a man in the dark. It's just my mother and I."

The sobbing continued from the other woman in the house. She sounded so heartbroken.

"I see. I'm going to take good care of you, Miss Fancy. I promise." Mrs. Winters lifted the sheet. "The babe is beginning to crown. It won't be long now."

"My mother. Please send word. She'll want to come."

"First things first, dear. Besides, I'm afraid I have no one to send at the moment. Now listen to what I tell you and this will go easier."

Fancy accepted a wet cloth the midwife handed her and held it to her sweat-drenched forehead. "I'll try."

Following every direction, Fancy did her utmost to ignore the agony and pushed as hard as she could when told. Not long after that, an odd sound met Fancy's ears as Judith Winters snipped the cord.

"I'll be right back." The midwife bustled out clutching a bundle in her arms.

Her baby. It wasn't crying. Fear froze the blood in Fancy's veins.

"What's wrong? Where are you taking my baby?" She lifted her head, panic flooding over her. "I want my baby! Please give me my baby!"

A young girl wearing a braid down her back entered. She looked to be maybe fourteen or fifteen. "My aunt said to tell you she'll be right back."

Fancy clutched the girl's arm. "Please tell me where she took my baby."

"I...it'll be okay." She pulled away from the bed and hurried out.

"My baby! I want my baby!" The sound of her yelling spread through the dwelling.

Finally, Mrs. Winters returned, wiping her hands on a towel. She lifted Fancy's hand, patting it. "Dear, I'm so very sorry. These things happen sometimes with no rhyme or reason."

"What things? I want my baby."

"Your son was stillborn. I wish I could change that, but I can't."

"No! No! I felt him move. He's not dead." Her shrill cries filled the room. "He can't be dead." She tried to rise but the midwife gently held her down.

"You can't get up yet. I know losing your child is a shock but maybe it was for the best. Cling to that," Mrs. Winters murmured.

"No!" Fancy shook her head from side to side in anguish. She heard the words, but they didn't register. Her panic turned into hysteria. "Let me see him!"

"I know how important it is to a mother to hold her child in her arms." Mrs. Winters seemed so understanding. The woman took her hand and patted it, her gentle words finally soaking into Fancy's head.

Her son was gone. He'd been there and in a hurry to see her then life had faded from his tiny body. An emptiness settled over Fancy's heart. Something shifted inside and instinctively she knew she'd never be the same again. Nothing would.

Mrs. Winters pulled a chair next to her. She wearily rubbed a hand over her eyes. "I tried to save him, but the cord was around his little neck and strangled him. Nothing I could do."

The sobbing ceased from the other person in the house. Had her baby died too?

Fancy stared at Mrs. Winters through a flood of tears. She'd sang and talked to her son for nine months and made plans.

The attack in the alley had happened so fast. The pain. The helplessness. The smell. The forceful way her son had been conceived. She'd tried to pretend it hadn't happened but the life growing inside soon proved the reality. The child was hers, and she loved him with every fiber of her being. She'd planned a wonderful future and things would've been so different.

Numbness set in as she wept. She'd lost a vital part of herself as though it had been chopped off. A hole formed where he'd been, one that would never close.

Gone. Just like her life. Fancy Dalton would never be whole again.

CHAPTER ONE

1881

A spring storm battered against the windows as thunder rattled the panes. Fancy sat by her mother's bedside applying a wet cloth to her feverish forehead, knowing in her heart the woman's time on earth would soon end.

A kindly old doctor long past his prime had just left. After checking Mama out, he'd confirmed what Fancy had already guessed. He'd patted her shoulder and said he wouldn't charge since he'd not done anything.

A sob tried to rise to give sound to Fancy's breaking heart. She swallowed hard to gain control of herself.

Once Mama bid the world goodbye, she'd truly be alone. Yet it already seemed she was.

For some strange reason, her thoughts chose to return to the child she'd never known, her stillborn son. He'd be two and a half now. She could almost see him toddling around on chubby legs, a big grin on his face. The years hadn't erased the pain of losing him. The baby had been so alive and brought such hope for the future. In the time she'd protected him inside her body and poured out boundless love, he'd become very real with his own personality. He hadn't even gotten a chance to take a first breath, let alone seen her face.

Fancy had promised that she'd always shield him from life's harshness. But she hadn't.

Her mother opened her eyes, her voice so weak Fancy could barely hear the words. "I'm not going to make it and I want you to be ready."

Mama worked her mouth, struggling to speak. "You have a smart head on your shoulders. And you're pretty. I couldn't afford to give you anything when you were born. Except your name. You looked like a fancy China doll." She licked her dry lips. "Your name should take you far."

"I love it. Thank you for giving it to me." In truth, she'd had to suffer men's crude suggestions and comments of what "fancy" seemed to mean to them, but she'd never once told her mother and never would.

A coughing fit gripped her mother. "You can make a good life for yourself." Her breath came in gasps. "Marry Abel Jordan. He'll provide for you."

Fancy gently dabbed flecks of blood from her mother's pale lips. "I don't love him." She'd rather be destitute than marry that disgusting man. "Don't worry about me. I'll be fine."

Abel Jordan's father owned the Whistle Stop Cafe where Fancy worked, and Abel would one day take it over. Business was booming, yet she never saw any of the profits. Mr. Jordan paid her nine dollars a month for waiting tables. But if he spied a customer tipping her, he'd deduct that amount from her salary and often make her give him the tip. He was nothing but a miserly skinflint.

And Abel...he leered and made crude remarks whenever

he strutted past. No, marriage to him was out even if he were the last person on the face of the earth.

Laying a fresh cloth on her mother's forehead, Fancy murmured, "Mama, you're not going to die, so stop thinking that. A little rest and you'll be fine."

Even as she said the words, she knew they were a lie, but she'd do anything to stave off the panic.

A flash of lightning illuminated the dim interior of the tiny two-room dwelling and a second later thunder shook the thin walls. A loud crash nearby said lightning must've struck a tree. Or someone's home although she prayed not. Storms scared her because they often carried destruction and death, but nothing frightened her more than losing the only person she had in the world. Mama had been her strength, her courage, her champion all her life. When she was gone, Fancy would be like a rudderless boat, drifting aimlessly.

Fancy wiped her eyes and pasted on a smile. "Do you know I saw the prettiest rainbow a few days ago over by the town square? It took my breath. They bring such hope."

Mama grimaced with the pain wracking her body. "When I was a little girl, I thought I could find a pot of gold at the end of a rainbow."

"We all want to believe in fairy tales." Fancy smoothed the soft, worn quilt. It was too bad such things never came true.

A knock sounded, and she went to crack the door open enough to peer out. "Yes?"

A shadowy woman stood in the deluge under an umbrella. With glittering eyes and a dark hood over her head, she looked frightening. "I'm looking for Fancy Dalton." Water poured off the caller's umbrella. "I was told she lives here."

Fancy hesitated for a moment, almost shutting the door. Finally, she spoke. "You've found her."

"Good. I have something to tell you."

What could this be about? It was horrible weather to go

calling. Before she could satisfy her curiosity, deafening thunder crashed around them.

"Won't you come in out of the storm?" she asked.

"I'd rather not. This is urgent and you'll want to hear what I have to say."

"All right." Fancy shivered in the cold, moist air. "I'm listening." Another flash of lightning illuminated the woman's face that looked vaguely familiar. "What is this about?"

"I've kept this secret long enough and I can't live with myself anymore." She hesitated for a second. "Your baby is alive."

Alive? Could it be true? A ripple of excitement raced through her.

The woman's anguished whisper raised the hair on Fancy's neck. "I did a horrible thing."

A knot formed in Fancy's stomach. "What do you mean? Because I never got to see my baby?" The midwife had told her that the sight of his little blue body would be too traumatic, so she'd never gotten a glimpse of the child she'd loved with all her heart and soul. Something she regretted to this day. Something she should've insisted on but had been too shaken and weak.

Suddenly, she recalled the shadowy face. And a name.

Judith Winters.

"I lied when I said your infant died in birth." Mrs. Winters pressed a piece of paper into Fancy's palm. "Here's the address where you can find him." The midwife took a deep breath as though to cleanse herself from the awful deed she'd done.

Fancy's legs tried to buckle, and she gripped the door. "Why? Why did you lie?"

"One of my patients…she'd experienced her third miscarriage that morning. She and her husband wanted a child so badly and could afford to give it a wonderful life. I could see how you loved your child but could give it very little."

"So you gave them my baby?" Fancy fumbled for words to express her fury. "You decided what was best? You and you alone? You lied to me!"

"Nothing I say will ever make it right."

"That's for certain." Unable to bear the pain of these developments, Fancy glanced down at her trembling hands. After a moment's silence, she met the woman's eyes. "Why now? Why tell the truth after two and a half excruciating years?"

"I can't live with it. Now, maybe I can finally sleep." Judith Winters whirled and disappeared into the rain before Fancy could ask anything else.

The woman had stolen her son and gave him away? Dear God. Tears ran down her face as she unfolded the piece of paper and read the names "Owen and Madeline Bishop." They had a Denver, Colorado address.

"Fancy?" her mother called weakly.

"Coming." She wiped her eyes, laid the precious scrap of paper on the small table, and hurried to her mother's bedside. "The most unbelievable gift came tonight." She told her mother about Mrs. Winters' confession. "He's alive."

Her mother clutched Fancy's arm with gnarled fingers. "You have to go. Go get your baby."

"How? It costs money. We barely live from day to day. Besides, you're sick."

"Don't worry about me." She gasped for breath. "My time…is almost…here." She dropped Fancy's hand. "Under the mattress. Money. Sell all our…belongings."

The reality that she might see her son burrowed into Fancy's heart like a bunny into a safe hole. Was it possible? She didn't even know the cost of a ticket to Denver. Yet, she'd get the money if she had to beg or borrow it.

Her son. He was alive. Somehow, someway she had to get

him back. Her arms ached to hold him. Mrs. Winters had scrawled a name on the note below the address—Daniel.

"Sweet, beautiful Daniel," Fancy whispered.

The midwife had also written out a confession and signed it. The stark statement sent ice through her veins. The woman had willfully stolen the child that Fancy loved with every fiber of her being. Then had the audacity to reason her actions away. Having no husband and little money had placed Fancy in the negative column.

Angry, she clenched her jaw so hard it made her teeth ache. She had to go after him and the urge to leave right then was overpowering.

But Mama…

CHAPTER TWO

Over the course of two days, her mother passed on and received a proper burial in a pauper's grave—against a stone wall of the old church where no grass grew. Mr. Jordan gave her a half day off. Evie, Fancy's best friend attended the burial to clutch her hand and give her strength.

With no living relatives left, she decided that Mama was right. She had to go fight for her child.

Despite grieving for the life she'd lost, Fancy set to work selling every stick of furniture, kitchen item, personal keepsake, and bedding article she could get a penny for. With her mother's seven dollars from under the mattress and what a group of neighbors had pitched in, she finally had enough for a train ticket and food. She'd seen a menu for the train and a hot biscuit and egg was thirty-five cents. So was soup. A biscuit by itself would suffice in a pinch.

She would need the little nest egg she had saved once she got to Denver.

Gathering the funds had taken two weeks. The only reservation available was on a Pullman train and it was only for a seat, not one of the comfortable sleeping compartments.

She'd make do and that would be fine. Knowing she'd soon see her baby Daniel again would make everything bearable.

She'd found great pleasure and satisfaction in giving her notice at the café and watching Mr. Jordan's mouth fall. Then she turned to Abel and spurned his offer of marriage in no uncertain terms. Anger turned his face purple.

In the two weeks of getting everything in order, she fretted at the time lost but knew she was doing her best. She visited Mama's grave every single day and talked to her. It brought comfort and she felt a loving spirit hovering around. Unseen hands seemed to smooth back her hair as Mama's voice whispered in her ear.

The day before her departure on the 1216 to Denver from nearby Council Bluffs, Iowa, Fancy stopped in to see her best friend and tell her goodbye.

Evie squealed and let her in, hugging her. "I'm so happy you're going on this wonderful adventure." She shifted the six-month-old in her arms. "You'll finally be able to see your son and hopefully hold him. The people raising Daniel have to let you have him back. He belongs to you. You have rights."

"I pray they'll see reason." Fancy chewed her lip. "But if they refuse, I don't know what I'll do. That possibility keeps me awake at night. After all, how can I prove he's mine? I only have the word of Mrs. Winters, and she'll be here in Saratoga. Besides, she lied before."

On top of that, Fancy would have no money for an attorney or to file papers. She pushed that out of her mind and reached for Evie's infant girl. Cuddling the sweet-smelling baby stilled some of the worry gripping her.

"I know there'll be something you can do. Someone to help you."

The world often showed little kindness to the poor still Fancy nodded. "How are you, Evie? Did Tom find work?"

Evie and Tom had only been married a year and like all

married couples they had their ups and downs. The main problem was Tom couldn't keep a job.

"He's working for Mr. Boroughs over at the gristmill and really likes it." Evie's face glowed. Hopefully, that would make a difference, and all would work out.

"That's wonderful." Fancy shifted the baby to her shoulder. "I swear this kid is growing by leaps and bounds. She's such a beautiful child."

Her eyes wide, little Mary tried to stick her fingers in Fancy's mouth. Fancy playfully nibbled at Mary's hand, drawing the child's heart-tugging laughter.

"I have something for you." Evie left the room and returned with a rose-colored dress and matching pretty hat. "This is slightly out of style, but I want you to have it. I gained so much weight with Mary, and I know I'll never be this small again. You'd look gorgeous in it, and you need something nice to wear on the train."

"Are you sure? I have no money to pay you."

Evie kissed her cheek. "I'm sure. My waist has stretched beyond redemption."

"The outfit is quite lovely. Thank you, dear friend." Fancy's throat closed up and her voice broke at the bleak prospect of never seeing Evie again. "I doubt I'll ever return to Saratoga. I really have nothing to come back to. I'm going to keep fighting until I get my son back, so I plan to get a job in Denver. Surely one of the cafés will need someone to wait tables. I'll scrub clothes if I must." She would do anything that would help get her child back.

Tears bubbled in Evie's eyes. "I can't stand the thought of that, Fancy. But I understand."

They talked a little more and Fancy put on the becoming hat. She took her leave, the pretty dress over her arm. She walked a few blocks to a cheap boardinghouse where she'd been staying since selling all their household belongings.

Since the woman had known her mother, she'd given Fancy a reduced rate.

The hours passed with Fancy growing more nervous by the minute. She spent the night restless, plagued by a multitude of doubts.

Had Mrs. Winters lied? Again?

Would the Bishops still live in Denver? They could've moved and this would be a wild goose chase.

If there, would they refuse to let her see her son?

And what about Daniel? What would he look like? Her? Or the horrible face of… She made herself stop. She wouldn't even think about that; whatever Daniel looked like was fine.

After tossing and turning all night, Fancy rose early and donned the dress Evie had given her, then packed all the belongings she had in the world into a worn carpetbag.

Whatever this trip held in store, it was beginning.

The Union Pacific depot in nearby Council Bluffs was a noisy hotbed of activity with travelers scurrying this way and that. The 1216 already sat idling on the tracks, plumes of white steam billowing around the big iron engine wheels.

Breathless, Fancy strolled to a window and bought a one-way ticket. She would refuse to check her bag, opting to keep it with her. Clutching the pass in one hand and her carpetbag in the other, she found an empty spot on a bench to wait until boarding time. A harried mother with a baby and two unruly boys sat beside her. They no sooner settled than the boys promptly ran off.

"Miss, would you hold my baby for a moment while I try to corral my boys?" Weariness lined the young woman's face. She probably wasn't much older than Fancy.

"Of course. But I'll need to board the train in a moment."

"I won't be long." The woman transferred the baby and

hurried across the room where the boys were scaling an iron railing.

When the scamps saw their mother coming, they jumped down and ran, knocking into rushing travelers. Just as their mother caught up to them, they darted out the door.

Oh dear. This could take a while. The baby glanced up at Fancy with wide eyes and burst into tears. Fancy rose, jiggling and talking to the babe until he hushed, all the while looking for the mother.

The conductor hollered, "All aboard!"

People grabbed whatever they had and filed out. Fancy bit her lip, scanning anxiously for signs of the missing mother but saw her nowhere. Within seconds, she was alone in the empty depot holding a strange child.

Fancy returned to the ticket window and explained the situation to the clerk. "I have to catch that train. It's very urgent."

The clerk peered over wire-rimmed glasses. "I'm sorry, miss. What do you want me to do? If you're suggesting I hold that child, the answer is no."

Hot tears stung the back of Fancy's eyes. "I must take this train."

"The conductor will issue a second boarding call before they leave. Pray she returns."

Disheartened, Fancy returned to her bag. A horrible stench rose up. She sniffed and found it came from the baby. The infant boy had filled his diaper. Great.

Each time Fancy heard a sound, she glanced toward the door. Just as the conductor issued the second call, the mother finally rushed in with the two boys in tow.

"I'm so sorry." Out of breath, she reached for the babe and wrinkled her nose. "Pew."

Fancy gave her a sympathetic smile. "I'd stay and help but I just have to get on that train."

Not waiting for more conversation or a chance for the

boys to run off again, Fancy grabbed her carpetbag and ran for the door. In her rush, she collided with a Stetson-wearing cowboy, a holster hanging from his lean hips.

He grabbed her, stopping her fall. "I'm sure sorry, miss. I'm hurrying to catch that train."

Fancy righted her hat and murmured, "Me too. I wasn't watching where I was going."

"Then let me get the door." A true gentleman, he held it for her, and they both sprinted for the train just as the conductor was removing the step.

"One moment, sir!" the cowboy yelled.

Her heart hammering, Fancy arrived gasping for breath. She set her bag down and fumbled in her pocket for the slim paper pass, handing it to the conductor.

"It's all right, miss," the kindly Union Pacific man assured her, reaching for the cowboy's ticket. "We won't leave you."

The conductor's neatly trimmed white hair, beard, and mustache gave him a distinguished look and made her think of a doting grandfather. His twinkling brown eyes gave her the impression that he loved life and people in general. A strange yearning filled her to lay her head on his shoulder and tell him about the son stolen from her and the mother she was still mourning. His age plus the kindness in his eyes and voice said she could trust him.

"I wasn't too certain about that." Fancy gave the man a wide smile. She held her skirt, grabbed her bag, and hurried into the crowded passenger car. However, a quick scan failed to yield an empty seat.

The cowboy's deep voice came from behind. "I believe there's a couple of vacancies on down."

True enough, she located them and took the inside, leaving her carpetbag in the aisle. She sank into the comfortable cushion, letting the cowboy have the aisle seat. Before he could pass her bag, a pimply-faced older boy possibly fourteen, rushed by and snatched it up. The thief continued toward the end of the car at a fast clip.

"Please stop him!" she cried, rising from her seat. "He stole my bag!"

Shaking uncontrollably, she watched her entire world disappearing through the door at the far end. The address in Denver of the people who had her son—gone. Everything gone. Just like that. And there was nothing she could do.

Without a word, the cowboy jumped up and gave chase. Passengers around her offered sympathy.

A double-chinned woman on the other side of the aisle clucked her tongue. "I don't know what this world is coming to. A decent person doesn't have a chance. The railroad needs to stop this riffraff." She turned to her daughter, a girl of about fourteen. "Mind your P's and Q's or you might wind up in jail just like this horrible boy when they catch him."

The girl sighed and rolled her eyes. "I know, Mama. I'm not stupid."

What a horrible thing to say to a daughter the woman should love.

Fancy smiled weakly and glanced toward the door at the far end for some sign of the returning cowboy but didn't see him. What-ifs ran through her head. Everything she possessed was gone, ripped from her. Her bottom lip quivered. What if she never recovered the bag? What would she do? How would she survive alone in a strange city? Her stomach clenched tight.

Stop it, she scolded herself. *Wait and see what happens before worrying about it.*

The dapper-looking conductor in his dark blue coat and pants stopped to talk to her. "I'm very sorry about the thief. When we catch the miscreant, we'll throw him off at the next town."

"Thank you, sir." She swallowed the lump in her throat. "I just pray you find my bag."

He patted her shoulder. "One thing about it, since we're moving, the boy and bag have to be on this train. We'll find them. I won't stop looking until we do. I've alerted all the employees to be on the lookout." He winked beneath thick brows. "We're very committed to our travelers. My name is Henry Manners. Call on me for anything."

"Thank you, Mr. Manners. You make me feel better. I'm Fancy Dalton."

"It's a pleasure serving you, Miss Dalton, and please call me Henry. I'll keep you informed on your stolen bag." He tipped his hat and went on.

As the iron wheels on the huge 1216 began to roll, Fancy sank back into the seat. She felt Henry's warmth around her and knew he'd move heaven and earth to help her. Evie had said she'd find help along the way, and she'd been right. Fancy closed her eyes a moment to settle her thoughts. She opened them as the cowboy was sliding into his seat.

"I didn't catch the wiry boy yet, miss, but I feel certain it's only a matter of time. The entire train has been alerted." He stretched out his hand. "I'd definitely say we're on speaking terms now. Jack Coltrain."

"Thank you, Mr. Coltrain."

He shook his head. "No, ma'am, I'm Jack."

"All right, Jack it is. Folks call me Fancy. Fancy Dalton." She took his hand and noticed the strength in his grip and calluses lining his palm. He evidently was used to strenuous work.

A grin curved his generous mouth. "Fancy, huh? That fits, if you don't mind me saying."

Whatever he was thinking, she sought to nip it in the bud. "I come from a long line of decent, honest, hardworking people. Until a few days ago, I served food in a small café."

"I didn't mean anything by that remark, Miss Dalton. I'm sure you hear it all."

"All and then some. Folks automatically assume the most

sordid things. The truth is, my mother knew she couldn't give me anything much in life except for a name that would stand out. What kind of work do you do, Jack?"

"My brother and I own a ranch outside of Omaha and run a good-sized herd of cattle." He opened his hands and inspected his palms. "I don't mind work. Or dirt. It's honest, as you said."

"Indeed, there is something to be said for that." She turned to look toward the far end of the car, hoping to see someone bringing her bag. But, of course, she didn't.

"It'll be all right, Miss Fancy. If I didn't have faith that someone will return with your bag, I'd go scour the train. As it is, I wouldn't know where to look. There seem to be a million places to hide something like that."

"What has me terrified is that the bag contains everything I own on this earth." She raised her gaze to his and found fascinating smoke-colored eyes studying her. "I had to sell every possession I had in order to make this trip to Denver."

"The journey must be important."

She clenched her resolute jaw. "A matter of the utmost importance."

"Then, I'll search until I turn it up. I remember what the bag looked like, and I'll find it," he promised.

That did nothing to reassure. The last person to promise her anything had stolen her child.

CHAPTER THREE

True to his word to the beautiful stranger, Jack Coltrain proceeded with a methodical search, checking every nook and cranny. He moved toward the back, swaying with the motion of the train, through each car with the rumbling of the wheels beneath him.

The boy had vanished through the far door, but he might've had an accomplice and passed the bag off. In that case, the booty could still be in the passenger car. However, after checking under and around every seat, it failed to turn up. Since the boy had run toward the front of the train, Jack ruled out the Pullman car behind them with its rich, polished wood and luxurious compartments.

Pushing on, he searched the parlor car where some of passengers were relaxing and playing a few cards. Some of the men indulged in a pipe or cigarette. No one had paid any attention to a boy carrying a bag.

The dining car had possibilities in the beginning, but Jack found nothing amiss there amid the beautifully set tables with small flower arrangements in the center of each. White jacketed porters moved silently, placing sparkling China and crystalware at each setting where soon the passengers would take a meal. Several of the porters glanced up and nodded. A few had noticed the boy racing through but again thought him just a wild ruffian.

The tables combined with the luscious smells coming from the kitchen area tempted Jack almost too much. As though on cue, his stomach growled. He'd been so busy pulling a calf this morning he hadn't eaten anything in his rush to make the train.

As it was, he'd almost missed the 1216. But to his way of thinking, it worked out like it had been ordained. If he'd arrived on time, he'd have missed meeting the lovely Fancy.

And that would definitely have been a shame.

She was quite a beauty all right with the most fetching shade of red hair. The strands were really more a soft coppery color, reminding him of the hide of the baby calf he'd helped into the world a few hours ago. Fancy's lovely brown eyes framed by long dark lashes were a perfect accompaniment for both her hair and the rose-hued dress she wore. He would've bet a year's pay she worked in the opera house singing her heart out to lonely cowboys.

The lady hid her lowly station in life very well. The pretty hat and white gloves helped.

Jack corralled his thoughts and hurried through the kitchen on to the baggage car. A large man wearing red suspenders glanced Jack's way. He clutched a small terrier with black, brown, and white patches. At sight of him the dog let out a soft whine and wagged its tail.

"I'm sorry to bother you, but I need to search in here for a bag a boy pilfered from a woman traveler," Jack explained. "She's quite distraught over the ordeal."

The man shook a mop of reddish hair out of his face. His eyes grew round. "I…I didn't take it."

"I'm sorry. I wasn't accusing you. I'm only trying to find it. It's a worn, purple and red carpetbag." Jack's attention strayed to a coffin against the wall of the car and a girl whose age he couldn't guess sitting with it. She turned red-rimmed eyes toward him and sniffled. He could say he'd ever seen anything quite so strange. He swung back to the red-haired baggage handler. "Did an older boy run in here with a bag like I just described?"

"It's just me an' Scruffy an' that little girl over there." The man scratched his head. "But I did see a boy. He shoved me an' was rude. Called me an imbecile. I think that's a bad word."

Jack shook his head. If he caught the thief, he was going to give him a lesson in manners.

"My name's Willie." The baggage man shifted the terrier and held out a dirty hand. "What's yours?"

"Jack. I'm glad to meet you, Willie."

While they were shaking hands, the wisp of a girl rose and came over. Now that she was closer, he thought her older than his first guess. "I saw the boy, mister. He stuffed the bag in the corner and put those large ones on top." She pointed and frowned. "He wasn't nice to Willie."

"The boy doesn't seem to have any couth." Jack went to the corner, and sure enough, under the stack set the carpetbag. He gave the girl wearing boy's trousers, suspenders, and shirt a smile. "Thank you for your help. Don't you think you need to go sit up with the passengers where it's more comfortable?"

"No, I need to be in here." She went back to her seat next to the coffin.

"Willie, it's been a pleasure meeting you." Jack patted the cute Yorkshire Terrier.

"I like having new friends." Willie scratched his head and Jack wondered if he had lice and when he'd washed it last. His hair and his hands.

"I'll come and say hello again before I get off." Jack went out and hurried to return the bag to its owner, anxious to put a smile on her pretty face.

Fancy saw him coming and leaped to her feet, throwing her arms around his neck. "I can't thank you enough. You've saved my life."

The faint scent of wildflowers surrounded him, reminding him of a spring meadow and fresh mountain stream. Fancy was different from anyone he'd ever met. There was something genuine, real, and unassuming about her that was missing in other women he'd known. The rough skin and broken nails on her delicate hands revealed signs of hard work, and the worn traveling bag told of her lowly station in life. No doubt the bag did hold everything she owned.

Thoughts of Jack's former lady friend, Margaret Warfield, flashed into mind. Margaret would've threatened to sue the Union Pacific, the conductor, and everyone else unless they produced her bag. Jack had once entertained a notion of marrying her—until he'd seen how spoiled and overbearing she was. Since then, he'd backed away, preferring bachelorhood.

Besides, it took time to court a woman, and he had little to spare. Until he and his brother got the ranch in better shape, it was his mistress.

Fancy pulled away. "I'm so sorry. I didn't mean to do that." Her face colored a becoming shade of pink. "I'm not one to go around throwing myself on strangers."

"No apology needed. You're just relieved."

"Yes, I am."

Before they sat down, the conductor interrupted with a young boy at his side. "I found the culprit, Miss Dalton. This young man has something to say, don't you, George?"

The angry boy glanced down. He was almost as tall as Fancy. "Sorry," he mumbled.

"That's not good enough, George." Henry shook him. "What's the rest? And say it like you mean it."

The thief's response was again mumbled. "I don't know what the fuss is about."

Henry gave George a hard shake. "You will know plenty soon, young man. Now apologize."

Sullen eyes looked up. "I'm sorry I took your bag, ma'am. Okay?"

Though clearly George was sorrier that he'd been caught, Henry led him away, saying he'd turn the boy over to the authorities at the next stop.

Fancy sat back in her seat and searched through the bag. "It seems to be all here."

"I don't think he had time to look inside before he hid it. I'm glad you didn't lose any of the contents. I had quite an unusual experience in the baggage car." Jack told her about the young girl beside the coffin and Willie.

"How sad. Did the girl say why she wouldn't leave the coffin?" Fancy asked.

"No, she just said she had to stay with it. Willie was watching over her. Maybe she felt more comfortable with the simple man and his dog."

"That breaks my heart. Poor child. She could be all alone in the world. I can relate to that." Fancy took a lace-edged handkerchief from the bag at her feet. "My mother recently passed, and she was all I had."

Jack patted her hand. "I'm sorry. I haven't had to go through that yet, thank God. The girl may be faced with a similar situation."

He glanced around the packed car and grinned at a toddler in front of them drooling spit over its mother's shoulder. A gentleman in a bowler hat nodded at him and a little girl with bows in her hair waved. He waved back. All were going somewhere for some reason.

"May I ask why you're going to Denver, Miss Fancy?"

"An important personal reason that will change my life and right a wrong. I can't say more than that."

"I see. Then I won't ask. I'm going to check out an ore mine that I recently inherited from an uncle." He ran a hand through his dark hair. "I don't know much about it, but I understand it's still operating. I hope it's producing. I can sure use a little working capital on the ranch that me and my brother own. We're close to going under if something doesn't change."

"A ranch probably takes a lot of money to run."

"It sure does, Miss Fancy. Between drought, more cattle than feed, disease, and any multitude of problems, we've never been flush. Just once before I die, I'd like to know what it's like to have enough." Or if that was just a pipe dream long told by cattlemen. He'd said too much. "I'm sorry. I didn't mean to burden you with my problems."

"I don't mind. Knowing what others face helps ease my own plight."

"You're too kind." He gave her a half-smile. "Would you excuse me? I want to stretch my legs and visit the parlor car. Maybe indulge in a game of cards if I can find another player." He stood. "They'll serve lunch in just a little bit. I'd count it as a favor if you'd dine with me."

"Of course. I'd be delighted."

Fancy's gaze followed Jack's six-foot figure as he moved down the aisle. He was certainly handsome with his dark, wavy hair and eyes the color of smoke. He must've spent a lot of time outside for the sun to have formed such deep lines at the corners of his eyes, especially when he smiled. Tall, lean men in boots and Stetsons captured her notice and Jack Coltrain had a way about him that she couldn't miss.

Unable to help herself, she leaned out of her seat a bit to see him better before she caught the prune-faced woman across from her staring and shaking her head. She quickly settled back.

A picture formed in her mind of Jack riding the range

and working with his cattle. Everything about him spoke of the land. His unhurried walk was like the gentle hills outside the train window. She'd seen storms in his eyes that said he'd seen his share of hard times and barely survived. Jack Coltrain would certainly be a man to have next to her when trouble came. But of course, their paths would separate once they got off the train in Denver and he'd go his own way.

Seemed everyone had problems of one kind or another and found it hard to hold on to what was most dear. She prayed he wouldn't lose his ranch. The world was a hard place, yet she was finding that when you had someone to share those difficulties with, the load seemed a lot lighter.

Fancy's thoughts turned to the girl in the baggage car. On impulse, she stood and grabbed her bag. She wouldn't feel right if she didn't try to convince the girl to sit with her.

The lady with two chins spoke from across the aisle. "Miss, if you want to leave your bag, I'll guard it with my life. I won't let anyone snatch it again."

It *was* rather bulky and hard to manage in the narrow aisle.

"Thank you. I'll only be a minute and I'd deeply appreciate it."

"Us women have to stick together. I'm Agatha. Mrs. Isaac Keegan III. And this is my daughter Alexandra."

Fancy introduced herself and spoke to the girl then moved the bag over to Agatha.

"And if your handsome gentleman should return, I'll do my best to keep him."

Fancy's face flamed. "You misunderstand, ma'am. He's not my anything. We just met."

Agatha winked. "Of course, dear. Anything you say."

Her daughter rolled her eyes. "Mother! Stop."

Embarrassed and a little bothered, Fancy hurried away from the busybody. While grateful to not have to worry about her bag, she'd do well to avoid Agatha and her kind. Maybe Henry would find her another seat.

Still perturbed, she moved down the rocking car, and when it went around a curve, she grabbed hold of whatever was available for balance.

White-coated waiters were working to put finishing touches to the tables in the dining car as she passed through. Fancy spoke and went on to the parlor car, noting a few folks playing cards, but Jack Coltrain wasn't one of them. Maybe he'd stepped outside on the metal platform to get some fresh air.

The train suddenly traveled a rough section of track and she had to clutch a door, proceeding slowly. In a few moments, it smoothed out and Fancy went into the baggage car. The noise was louder here. The red-haired gentleman must be Willie that Jack mentioned.

Her gaze went to the little girl sitting next to the coffin before she introduced herself to Willie. "I wanted to come and see if I can be of assistance. I know how loneliness can be."

"Yes, ma'am." Willie appeared uncomfortable, smoothing his wild hair. "I don't think I've seen anyone as pretty as you, Miss Fancy." He turned to the girl. "Have you, Piper?"

The child rose and came over. "I agree, Willie. She's pretty."

"Piper. How unusual." Fancy admired the girl's pretty eyes and long blond braids.

"My mama liked the name," she said softly. "I guess yours liked Fancy."

"As a matter of fact, she thought 'Fancy' sounded like a person with money. We were so poor." Fancy glanced at the coffin. "I assume that's your mother?"

"I promised I wouldn't leave her side." Piper's green eyes filled with tears and her lip quivered. "I'm taking her to Denver to be buried in the mountains. She loved them so."

"I can see why. Is anyone meeting you?"

Piper shrugged and turned back to her chair. "I dunno. Maybe."

Fancy took in the trousers and suspenders, wondering if Piper owned a dress. "Would you like to talk a moment? We have a lot in common. I lost my mother recently and feel so alone."

"I guess you can sit on a trunk, cain't she, Willie?"

The baggage handler took out a neckerchief and dusted the trunk off then dragged it over. "Here you go, ma'am."

Fancy thanked him and sat down, hoping she wouldn't fall off if the train went around a curve. The little Yorkshire terrier rose from a box lined with scraps of soft blankets. The dog stared and stretched, yawning.

"Did you have a good snooze, Scruffy?" Willie picked his pet up. "You're my little boy."

How sweet to see the love Willie showered on the pet. Likely, the dog was all he had.

"Henry said I could keep Scruffy on the train if I kept him in here with me. We ain't allowed to go up with the passengers." Willie kissed the sweet dog on the nose. "But we don't care. This is a good home for Scruffy and me."

"Indeed it is, Willie." Fancy reached to touch the little dog's soft snout, and he licked her fingers. "He's certainly a cute pup."

A hammock was stretched in the corner, and she assumed Willie slept there. Piper must sleep on the floor or atop the coffin. How sad. And she didn't know if anyone was meeting the girl or not. Suddenly, Fancy's situation didn't seem quite as dire.

"How old are you, Piper?"

"Twelve. But I know how to get by."

With the girl's slight frame, Fancy would've guessed her much younger. "I'm sure you do. Who's really meeting you in Denver?"

"A grandfather, I guess. I don't know him, and he don't

know me. My mama didn't like him much. They had a falling out when she left. He's probably mean."

"Honey, don't think that. He might be very nice. What about your grandmother?"

Piper shrugged again. "Dunno. Mama said she lets Grandfather rule things." Her small chin raised at a defiant angle. "Well, I don't need 'em. I'll see to Mama and leave."

"And go where, honey? Do you have other relatives?"

"I don't need anyone. I'm twelve and can make my own way."

"That'll be hard." Fancy didn't tell her how impossible that would be. "If you'd like, I can go with you to meet your grandparents so you won't have to face them alone. It's scary."

"You'd do that for a strange kid?" The girl's eyes widened. "For me?"

Fancy put an arm around Piper's thin shoulders. "Yes, for you, honey."

Tears burned the back of Fancy's eyes. She'd want someone to do that for her son. To be there to feed and care for him through long, cold nights.

All of a sudden, the need to be in Denver, to see her baby, hug him burned through her like an unquenchable wildfire.

For the first time, she allowed herself to picture Daniel in her mind. He'd have light red curls, a shy smile, and curious blue eyes. He'd reach for her and say, "Mama."

A tremble raced through Fancy, and she pushed that daydream aside. Everyone knew dreams never came true and the fear she might never see him was all too real. She dragged her attention back to Piper. "When did you last eat?"

The girl frowned and shrugged. "Don't remember."

Conscious of her low funds that she'd have to stretch, Fancy quickly decided that she could do without so the girl could have sustenance. Then, it dawned on her that Jack had invited her to eat with him. She prayed he wouldn't mind one extra, but if he did, she would decline the invitation. Piper's needs would come first.

Fancy smiled, smoothing the girl's hair. "Then you must be hungry. The dining car will be open soon. Let's find a place to wash up."

Willie grinned. "Piper, go eat."

"Okay." The girl raised obstinate eyes. "Then I'm coming right back. I won't leave Mama for long. She needs me. She's scared of the dark."

"I'll watch over her," Willie promised.

Fancy swallowed a lump in her throat. Clearly, the girl felt a duty to protect her mother—even in death.

CHAPTER FOUR

The train stopped at the town of Columbus to let folks on and off and take on coal and water. Fancy had no desire to leave the train. She peered through her window as Conductor Henry turned the thief George over to a lawman. She felt sorry for the boy but maybe this would teach him something and steer him from a life of crime. Lessons were hard and law breaking came with consequences.

With Piper in tow, Fancy found a small washroom placed at the back of the car. She was waiting outside the door when she spied Jack coming toward her and waved.

"There you are. The woman across the aisle from you said you were on a mysterious errand and implied you might be meeting a lover." His gray eyes twinkled. "I wasn't sure what she meant."

"Some folks like to stir the pot to see what rises to the top." Fancy released a tired sigh. "Seems they have nothing better to do. I assure you, I don't have a lover. I'm actually waiting for the girl from the baggage car to come out of the washroom. Her name is Piper, no last name yet." Speaking quietly, Fancy told him all she'd learned about the girl's situation. "I feel so sorry for her. She's lost the one person she can trust and is scared of meeting these grandparents who disowned their daughter. Who knows the last time she's eaten so I convinced her to come with me. I don't know how you feel about it after inviting me to eat with you but..." She hesitated.

Jack's smile revealed a row of white teeth. "Actually, I wanted to find you to see if we could talk to the girl and feed her. There's no problem at all. With two lovely ladies, I'll be the envy of the dining car."

A little strand of black hair fell onto his forehead and gave him a rather rakish look. Fancy's heart fluttered softly. Another time under different circumstances, she might've welcomed his attention. But she wouldn't let anything distract her from finding Daniel. Not even the handsome, debonair Jack Coltrain.

"Thank you, Jack. I'm so happy you feel that way."

He shrugged. "What kind of man would I be if I didn't? I'll go back to our seats to wait for you ladies."

"Thank you. Try to avoid Agatha."

"I'll feed her a line of bull she'll have trouble swallowing."

He turned toward the seats and Fancy's gaze followed him. He cut such an eye-catching figure. Lean waist and long legs were all pluses. But the thing that really drew her was his lack of pretense. He didn't pretend to be someone he wasn't. That was rare among the men she'd known.

Piper emerged and actually smiled. "Thank you, Miss Fancy. I feel better."

"I'm glad. Would you like me to fix your hair or at least straighten it up?"

"Mama loved doing that." Tears again filled Piper's eyes. "I think I'd like you to fix it."

They returned to the baggage car and Piper dug a brush from her small bag. Willie and Scruffy watched as Fancy worked magic on the girl's hair.

"It feels like Mama's back there," Piper murmured, sniffling. She turned and flung herself into Fancy's arms. "I don't know what I'll do, Miss Fancy."

"Honey, this has to be the hardest thing you'll ever face. I wish I could make it easier." She hugged the grief-stricken child and murmured soothing words.

The next thing she knew, Willie was sobbing as well and Scruffy whined pitifully. Good heavens. Fancy took a handkerchief from her pocket and passed it around so they could all dry their tears. After finishing Piper's hair, Fancy adjusted the beautiful hat Evie had given her, and they left to find Jack.

He was waiting at the dining car door, her bag in hand. "There you are. I knew you wouldn't want to leave your belongings."

"Bless you, Jack. I'm truly grateful." Fancy turned. "Piper, this is Jack Coltrain."

"He's nice. He came into the baggage car looking for your bag." Piper slipped her small hand in his. "I showed him where it was."

Jack gave her a grin. "And you don't know how much I appreciated your help, young lady." He removed his hat and ushered them to a table, pulling out chairs for both, acting the perfect gentleman. Before he sat, Jack placed his hat on the extra seat, crown down.

The porter poured water, inquired how they were liking the trip, and took their order.

The choice was easy for Fancy. She chose the cheapest thing on the menu, and Piper followed her lead. Jack made it unanimous except for his coffee.

Over a fine meal of broiled ham and vegetables, they discovered Piper's last name was O'Connor as well as her grandparents.

"Could your grandfather be Declan O'Connor?" Jack asked.

Piper gave her trademark shrug. "Don't know."

"Why, Jack?" Fancy asked. "Do you know a Declan O'Connor?"

"He's the man I'm going to see." Jack helped Piper cut her ham. "Would your grandfather be in the mining business?"

"I don't know anything about him." She crossed her arms. "And I don't care to learn. He hates me."

"Are you sure?" Jack asked softly. "Can you give him a chance? You might be surprised if you open your heart."

"He made Mama cry, and she said he didn't want her. Well, he don't want me either. She said so." Piper gripped her fork so hard, her knuckles turned white.

Why would a mother tell her child such things? Especially knowing she wouldn't have long to live. Making the gulf even wider between her parents and her daughter was a terrible thing to do.

Fancy patted Piper's hand. "That's not quite fair. As Jack said, they might surprise you." Seeing the distress this line of conversation caused, Fancy glanced out the window at a flock of birds flying in a V. "Now, where do you suppose those birds are going?"

Piper slipped out of her chair and pressed against the glass. "I think they're coming from the south. Mama said they go there for the winter and spend summer in the north. The mamas probably had some babies." She touched her hand to the glass. "I wish I could fly away with them."

Across the table from Fancy, Jack lifted an eyebrow.

Just then, the bird at the tail end on the left dipped low.

"Oh no! It's falling," Piper cried. "Help it."

"Honey, we can't do anything." Fancy rubbed her shoulder. "Even if we were outside, we couldn't reach up there to the sky."

"But—" The distraught girl turned back to see another bird fly beneath the tired one and lift it back up. "Oh, the mama bird got it. She's helping it fly."

Fancy blinked hard. That was what mamas did for their children. They were there to lend a hand and show their children how to fly. What would Piper do now without her mother for love and support? Or Fancy herself? Though older, she was also alone and having to make her way. She desperately needed her mother.

But now it was her turn and with a miracle, she would get a chance to teach Daniel.

The birds flew on and Piper sat back down. The girl talked about happier times and how she'd taken care of her mother even by age six. It became apparent from her stories that the roles had reversed, and the mother had become the child. In reading between the lines, Fancy learned that problems had apparently depressed the woman, so she hadn't even tried to deal with them. Or see that Piper was fed or went to school. Her mother had taken to her bed a lot and pulled the covers over her head.

"It wasn't Mama's fault though," Piper said defending her mother. "She loved me. She couldn't help being sick."

"No, of course not, honey." But the woman shouldn't have shifted everything to her young daughter.

Piper stared at the white tablecloth and traced a design with her finger. "Mama was just different. But she loved me. She really loved me. And sometimes we'd lie in bed, and she'd tell me about the handsome prince that rode away on a white stallion or about life in a castle." Piper raised sad eyes. "I knew it was only pretending, but I didn't care. She was happy. And that was enough."

Jack covered her hand. "Hold fast to the memories, kiddo. They stay with us no matter what and help us over the rough times."

The porter came for their dishes and Jack ordered apple pie all around, refusing to listen to Fancy saying she was too full.

"You didn't take us to raise, Jack," she protested. "This was only a dinner invitation."

"Hush." The dark-haired charmer's lopsided grin made her breath catch. "I haven't eaten with two lovely ladies in a long while and I don't want it to end."

She couldn't help but return his smile. "Do you practice your sweet-talking on your cows?"

"They don't mind a bit."

His grin and the way he looked at her did funny things to Fancy's stomach.

"Cows?" Piper's eyes lit up. "You have cows?"

At his nod, the child asked a million questions about ranching and Jack's herd. And for a little while the sadness left her eyes.

The pie came and they ate their fill. Fancy's stomach hadn't gotten this much food in quite a while. It felt a little odd to not feel hunger pangs. She suspected it was the same for Piper. No telling when the girl ate last or how filling it had been.

After the meal, Piper stood and scooted her chair in. "Mama needs me. She'll be upset," she said and went back to the baggage car.

Fancy watched her go. "I just want to cry, Jack. She hasn't ever gotten to be a child."

"Doesn't sound like it. And now Piper *still* has to take care of her mama." He gathered Fancy's bag from under the table. "While I was exploring a little earlier, I found a small alcove off the parlor car that offers a breathtaking view. Would you like to see?"

"Let me think about this." She glanced up into his smoky eyes. "I could go with you and enjoy the view. Or I could go back to my seat and get another dose of busybody Agatha?" A chuckle escaped. "There's no comparison."

"Are you sure? Who knows what dear Agatha has cooked up by now."

"That's what I'm afraid of." Giggling, Fancy held her skirt and went through the doorway. She hadn't felt this lighthearted in years.

For just a few moments, she could set her worry and uncertainty aside.

The little alcove was everything Jack claimed. Even a portion of the ceiling was glass that allowed her to see the sky. The best part was that this area of the car was vacant.

"This is really nice." She settled into a comfortable chair, her bag at her feet. She'd once traveled by train to Lincoln, Nebraska—a whole whopping fifty miles—but it was nothing like this. She was beginning to get used to the rumble of the wheels under her feet and the sound of the whistle at each crossing and town depot.

And Jack. He was interesting.

Jack sat across from this woman who'd captivated him. Her rich, earthy brown eyes held sorrow. "I thought you might like the peace of this little space." He motioned to the patch of blue sky through the window overhead. "Not a cloud in sight. We shouldn't experience any delays."

"For that I'm grateful. I'm in a hurry to reach my destination. Have you traveled much?"

"I've been to Denver several times to visit Uncle Anson and also trips around Nebraska. Coltrains are scattered near and far like the seeds of a dandelion." He chuckled. "You?"

"I once took a fifty-mile trip once to Lincoln. Mama and I stayed close to home."

"I notice you use the past tense."

She nodded. "I buried Mama two weeks ago. She took ill and couldn't recover."

"That's why you seem to relate to Piper so well. You're still in mourning."

"I know some of what she's going through, although, because of her young age, her grief is much deeper. The unknown is such a scary place and even more when you haven't the ability to provide for yourself. She's really at the mercy of her grandparents and knowing that frightens her to death. Her mother didn't help pave the way any there and that's a pity."

"It sure is. It's like the mother was jealous of any feelings Piper might develop for them. I've seen this before where the child had to raise the parent and it wasn't pretty." Memories of the family that lived down the road from Jack filled his thoughts. The mother had kept her child away from anything normal and good by imaginary health concerns.

"All I know is that I'm not going to let that child face her grandparents alone. I will be there to help, and bury her mother." Fancy's statement rang with determination.

"If you don't mind, I'd like to be by your side." He was quiet a moment. "Wouldn't it be an odd twist of circumstances if her grandfather is the Declan O'Connor I'm going to see?"

"It would be mighty strange but I'm sure there are lots of O'Connors in the world." Fancy moved closer to the window to peer at the passing scenery.

The countryside was awash in color with spring flowers everywhere and trees putting on leaves. Jack took advantage of her distraction to look his fill. She had the most delicate, shell-like ears and the tiny pearl earrings she wore were perfect with her skin coloring. The fringe of long lashes provided a dark frame for her eyes. And her dainty hands were accustomed to work.

"Do you know what I thought when I first saw you?" he asked quietly.

She swung a curious gaze at him. "No, what?"

"The way you carried yourself and your eye-catching

beauty seemed befitting for an opera singer or a woman of the stage. I was certain."

Soft laughter sprang from Fancy's mouth. "Jack, you are so funny. I wait tables for a living. And before that, I worked in a laundry, scrubbing clothes. I've never been anything close to an opera singer or actress."

"I can't help what I think. Your mother was right. 'Fancy' suits you. What are you going to do in Denver if I might ask? You mentioned trying to right a wrong."

"Something was stolen from me, and I have to get it back. Not sure yet how."

He studied her a moment, wondering what had happened to make her so dead set on leaving everything behind and going in search of this something. "If you need help or moral support, I'll be happy to back you up."

"Thank you." She looked at him and teased softly, "Are you the 'help a damsel in distress' kind of cowboy?"

"I'm anything you want me to be, pretty lady. And I'm dead serious."

Her laughter died. "Yes, I can see that. I will call on you should I need assistance."

Jack scribbled on the back of a card and handed it to her. "These people will know how to find me."

Fancy stuck the card into her bag. "Thanks. Tell me more about your ranch. You mentioned that you need capital."

"That's right." Jack leaned back in the chair and stuck his long legs out in front of him. "I don't know why I'm telling you this, but truth is, we're in serious trouble. This land has been in our family for five generations, and we stand to lose it all." He rubbed his face with his hands. "If we can't find the money to pay off the bank, we'll lose everything."

"I'm sorry. Can't you sell the cattle?"

"The bottom dropped out of the market. What little we'd get wouldn't be enough."

"Then I hope Denver provides your answers."

"Actually, my uncle's mine is in a new area called Cripple Creek. Once I get to Denver, I'll ride up the mountain to Uncle Anson's." Jack lowered his voice. "He sent my brother and I a letter a while back saying he found something exciting. But he didn't want to say what for fear of word getting out. Then we got a notice two weeks ago from Declan O'Connor in Denver notifying us he'd died and to come soon."

"What are you thinking, Jack?"

"I'm not sure. All I know is that I have to get there and find out."

"Did O'Connor explain his relation to your uncle? Is he a lawyer?"

"A friend. He owns the mine next to Uncle Anson's but offered nothing more. I can't help thinking that he knows a lot that he didn't say. Like all miners, he's playing his cards close to his chest. They have to be wary of everyone or lose it to thieves." Jack released a troubled sigh. "I guess I'll find out when I get there."

Everyone had more than one reason to reach their destination. He took Fancy's measure again and noted the sheer determination on her face. The pretty woman had more than enough strength to find whatever had been stolen from her. But he had the suspicion that this item in Denver was far more important than a bag full of belongings.

Jack was more than happy to be by her side. Maybe all they'd have was just friendship, and, if so, that would satisfy him. But maybe with luck, this new relationship would turn into a bit more with a little help from above.

For a start, he'd find Henry Manners and see if the conductor would locate her a seat away from the irritating Agatha.

CHAPTER FIVE

The little alcove had filled her with a kind of peace and had loosened the knots between her shoulders but now she was weary, the frantic day catching up with her.

Fancy covered a yawn. "This has been lovely, Jack, but I think I need to return to my seat. I'm a little tired." Fancy rose and reached for her bag.

"Wait a moment." Jack stood and waved the conductor over as he was walking past. "Henry, were you able to find Miss Dalton a different seat?"

"Not exactly. But I think I can resolve the problem to everyone's satisfaction if you'll just give me a moment." He smiled and took Fancy's bag. "Let me assist you to your seat, and I'll work my magic."

"I'll be along in a little while." Jack moved aside for a fellow traveler. "I have to check on my horse in the stockcar."

Fancy nodded and followed Henry back to the passenger car.

Agatha was knitting, her needles moving as fast as her mouth. Her poor daughter's eyes had glazed over. "There you are, Miss Dalton. I wasn't sure what happened to you. Sometimes people have been known to disappear on these trains. Why, I've had several no more than sit down than they vanished. But of course—"

Henry jumped in as she took a breath. "Excuse me, Mrs. Keegan, I wondered if perhaps you were a little bored in this seat. I have a special one for our regular passengers in the Pullman car that is very plush. We keep it saved so we can provide a little extra service for important people like you." When Agatha's attention shifted to her daughter, Henry winked at Fancy.

"Well, I do go back and forth a lot. Yes, we'll take it." Agatha began to stuff her knitting into a bag. "I'm glad you finally recognize who I am. My husband is very important."

Fancy watched the exchange, hard pressed to contain laughter.

"Yes, ma'am. Mr. Keegan III is a real influential man in Nebraska," Henry answered.

In no time, Agatha and her daughter were moving down the aisle with Henry, and Fancy was left to peace and blessed quiet. She rested her head against the back of the seat and closed her eyes. The morning had exhausted her. And she needed to plan her arrival. She decided to go slowly even though she itched to go directly to her son and clasp him close to her.

Piper complicated things a bit. Fancy would first have to make sure the grandparents would take the girl before she left her. If they didn't, she would have to step in. Leaving Piper on her own in a city of Denver's size was out of the question. That could be disastrous.

The clickety clack of the wheels lured Fancy to sleep. She jolted awake when the train slowed, sounding its whistle. They must be pulling into another station. She glanced out the window to see the train was coasting into a sea of cattle. Must be hundreds.

Worry lining his face, Henry hurried down the aisle. "Do you know where I might find Mr. Coltrain?"

"Is there trouble?" Maybe the train was being held up.

"We're not in any danger, if that's what you mean. It's those cattle outside."

That was sure to cause a delay, but for how long?

"Did you check the alcove in the parlor car? Or the stock car?"

"Not yet. I'm on my way there. We need his services, or we'll be stuck here for a while."

"I'll come with you." She grabbed Jack's Stetson off the other seat and glanced at her bag.

"I won't let anyone bother it," a friendly woman sitting behind her said. "It'll be safe."

With that assurance, Fancy fell in behind Henry as the train came to a complete stop.

They hurried on with Henry speaking, "Mrs. Keegan is very happy in her new compartment. I gave her a whistle and the job of alerting the passengers in the event outlaws come aboard. She seemed impressed."

"That's good. I feel badly for asking you to move her."

"You didn't. Mr. Coltrain did, and it was no difficult task. She's as happy as a lark."

Luck would have it that Jack was in the alcove. He'd stretched out and was fast asleep.

Henry shook him awake. "Mr. Coltrain, a herd of cows have surrounded the train, and unless we move them, we'll have to spend the night here."

Jack scrubbed his face with his hands. "I'll see what I can do, but I need a horse. Mine has a gash on his leg. Appears he fell into a jagged board when the train went around a curve or something."

"Oh dear." Worry deepened the lines of Henry's face.

"There were two others in the car, but they look like high-dollar racehorses."

Henry brightened. "Coltrain, if you can use one of those,

I'll find out who they belong to." He rushed off to check his passenger list.

"You might need this too." Fancy handed Jack the Stetson.

"Thanks. I'll feel more normal." He put it on. "A racehorse?" Jack chuckled. "I guess I can try it, but those are a totally different breed. Most are very high strung."

Fancy glanced out the window and there appeared to be even more cattle than before. "Jack, can one man corral all those cows by himself?"

"Not usually and it'd be hard even if I could ride my horse. But a race animal that's bred for speed? This could be a disaster."

"Look, Jack. There's a woman out there afoot, doing her best to move the cattle. She's waving what looks like an apron."

"Good Lord!" He squeezed in next to her. "She'll never herd them that way." He took Fancy's hand. "Come on, let's go open the baggage door and talk to her."

They hurried forward and Willie slid the door open. Piper joined them.

Jack leaned out. "Ma'am, why aren't you on a horse?"

The woman came closer. "My husband hitched our horses to a wagon and went into town with our two hired hands. Won't be back until tomorrow. I have nothing to ride. When I saw the downed fence, I ran after the herd. I'm so sorry."

"Hold on and stay out of the way of those horns and hooves," Jack said. "I'll round them up for you as soon as I find a horse to ride. The conductor should be back any second."

"Oh, thank you!" Sweat running down her face, the woman came over to the car. She looked to be middle-aged with gray streaks in her hair. "I'm at my wit's end."

"Take a deep breath," Fancy encouraged as she and Piper sat in the open door. "Help is on the way. How far do you live from here?"

"About five miles. My husband and I settled here twenty years ago and watched the workers lay the tracks that cut right through our property. I'm Madge Browning."

Jack sat down next to Fancy. "Those tent towns must've been wild, Mrs. Browning."

"Gunplay every night. We were glad to see them move on." She wiped her brow with the back of a hand.

Henry appeared with a droopy-eyed man wearing a little bowler hat. "This here is Mr. Sweeney. He's the handler of the racehorses."

Sweeney grinned and talked in a slow drawl. "This'll be quite a sight, and the horses won't know what to think. Still, seeing as how we're stuck here until the cattle are moved, you're welcome to try to ride one. But injure them and my boss will have your hide and mine both."

"Of course. Do you know how to herd cows, Sweeney?" Jack peered at him. "It's really a job for three at least."

"Nope. Sorry."

"Care to give it a try?" Henry asked.

"Nope. I sure wouldn't."

Fancy could've poked the sleepy-eyed man with a pin. He could at least give it a shot. She spoke up, "I've never done it either, Jack, but I can follow instructions. We have to get this train moving."

"That's for sure, ma'am." Henry gave her a grateful smile.

The cattle's owner had strength in her features. "I've herded a lot and don't mind giving you a hand. Not too sure about doing it astride a racehorse though."

"Thank you, ma'am." Relief bathed Henry's face. "Come down to the stockcar next door and we'll get the horses unloaded."

Jack got to his feet and the men filed out.

Fancy was more than a little relieved that she wouldn't have to help. "Let's sit right here, Piper. We have a good seat."

The girl glanced up at Fancy, grinning. "I'm so excited to watch Mr. Coltrain round these up. I think he can do most anything. Don't you?"

Piper O'Connor had more than a little case of hero worship it seemed.

"Yes, dear. I think he's very good at anything he does." Fancy was glad Jack didn't hear her say that. In her experience, it was never good to let a man know what a woman was thinking.

In no time, Jack and Sweeney led the horses down the ramp. Only one wore a funny looking saddle, the other had none.

"Let me try this out before I turn the horse over to you," Jack told Madge Browning. He swung into the saddle and rode the skittish animal a little way, its graceful legs eating up the ground. Jack turned and came back, skimming across the distance in nothing flat.

The horse was mighty spirited, and Fancy could see the strength it took to restrain the animal. She prayed Madge could handle it. But her main fear was for Jack. His horse would have no saddle or reins, therefore no way to stay on.

Jack dismounted. "Mrs. Browning, you'll need a firm hand, but you should be fine."

"I'll do my best." The cattle's owner stuck her foot in the stirrup, threw a leg over and settled into the leather seat.

Then Jack went to the second thoroughbred that Sweeney held by a lead rope. Fancy clutched Piper's hand as he gripped the mane and easily leaped onto the horse's glistening back.

As soon as the animal felt Jack's weight, it took off running with him hanging on for dear life. His hat flew off and the excited horse stomped on it. The cows scattered this way and that to avoid a collision. Fancy's heart was in her throat. She closed her eyes, unable to watch.

There was going to be blood spilled. Hopefully just a little bit, but chances were a lot.

Next to her, Piper was hollering encouragement at the top of her voice. The child wouldn't have any lungs left. "Watch him go! You're so brave, Mr. Coltrain! You can sure ride!" Then she yelled, "Oh no!"

"What?" Fancy's eyes flew open. Jack had slid sideways on the galloping animal, right through the herd again scattering them. He righted himself quickly. "Hold on!" Fancy screamed as he flew by.

Finally, the horse settled down and she could breathe a sigh of relief. Somehow or another he got the animal under control and he and Madge set to work, both keeping a tight grip on the horses. At times, the mounts still got away from the pair, but their running streaks were quickly curtailed.

Slowly, the pair managed to gather the herd into one large cluster and got them headed toward the downed fence.

"Henry, will there be other trains through here after us?" Fancy asked.

"Yes, I'm afraid so, and I share your worry. What will keep the cattle inside the fence with it down? I don't have an answer for that. We can telegraph a warning but that's about it."

"That'll have to do I suppose."

Twilight had fallen by the time Jack rode back with the second horse in tow. Fancy was in the dining car eating with Piper, listening to the girl sing Jack Coltrain's praises. He was a full-fledged cowboy and could ride a wild horse using no reins according to Piper. Then it became galloping with no hands and Fancy rolled her eyes.

When he entered the car, people stopped to stare. One shirt sleeve hung in shreds, his trousers were ripped and had Fancy couldn't tell what color they used to be. The brim of his hat was bent at a funny angle. He respectfully removed the stomped Stetson at the door.

Fancy got to her feet. "Jack, I'm glad you're back. Piper and I were very worried. Are you okay? Do you need a doctor?"

"I'm fine, but my nerves are wound tight." He pulled out a chair and sat, laying his hat in a vacant seat.

The porter was there in an instant, and Jack ordered his food, adding, "I'd really like a cup of coffee right away please."

"Excellent, sir. Coming right up." The porter hurried off.

"Mr. Coltrain, you were amazing." Piper propped her elbows on the table and leaned closer. "How did you stay on?"

"I just held tight and prayed a lot." Jack grinned. "Actually, the horse was great once it figured out what I wanted it to do and learned to dawdle but it didn't much like to mosey."

"I'm sure not." Fancy laughed. "I wish someone could've taken your picture. That was priceless. Why did it take you so long to ride back?"

"It wouldn't have done much good putting them in the same pasture as the downed fence, so Mrs. Browning and I took them to another and made sure the fences were sound."

With him a cattleman, she should've known he'd think of everything.

"That's good. Henry and I were worried about the trains coming behind us. He'll be relieved."

"I just spoke to him." Jack took the cup of coffee from the porter.

"Can you teach me to ride like that?" Piper asked. "After I bury Mama, I could join a Wild West show and be a trick rider. I wouldn't have to live with my grandfather."

Fancy tried to contain laughter but a chuckle escaped. "That's some dream, Piper."

"Maybe you better finish growing up first, girl." Jack

ruffled her hair. "But I could teach you to ride once we get to Denver—on a doddling old gray mare."

She didn't seem to hear the old gray mare part. Her eyes grew wide. "You mean it?"

"Sure thing, kid. But first I'll have to see to the gash on my gelding's leg." Worry clouded his gray eyes.

"Do you think he'll be all right?" Fancy asked.

"Depends on if the tendons are cut. If so, I'll have to put him down."

"Kill him?" Alarm made Piper's voice shrill. "Why? You can't!"

"Honey, if the tendons were severed in the accident, he'll likely be unable to walk." He patted her hand. "Let's cross that bridge when we get the facts. For now, I've bandaged it and he doesn't seem in too much pain. That's a good sign."

"We'll pray he'll get well." Fancy couldn't help but worry. It was really sad when animals got injured. "What is his name, Jack?"

"Reno. I raised him from a colt. His mother Morning Dawn was the best cow horse I ever saw. She could read my mind."

"I like that. Reno." Piper sat back with a smug expression. "Reno is going to be just fine and his leg will heal. You just wait."

Jack nodded. "How's that sky out the window for a beautiful sunset?"

Fancy sucked in a breath. Brilliant streaks of purple, blue, red, orange, and yellow colored the panoramic view, blending and swirling together. With every blink of her eye it changed into something even more beautiful. "That's really spectacular. Like God put on a show just for us."

"That's what I was thinking." Jack spoke softly, met her gaze, and held it. Try as she might, Fancy was unable to look away.

What did this mean? Why now after all these years of loneliness and a mountain of heartache?

Jack excused himself and went to change into a clean shirt. Just then the wheels of train 1216 began to roll once more. Now they had one more reason to get to Denver. They had a horse to doctor and Fancy to keep her head.

CHAPTER SIX

As darkness descended, Fancy thought of Piper in the baggage car with Willie and the little terrier. Despite the excitement of Jack's cattle-herding that had perked her up, the girl still refused to leave her mother. Not even to come sit with Fancy for a while.

But there was little she could do to change Piper's mind.

Fancy yawned. The passengers in the Pullman Car must be getting ready to sleep in their compartments. With curtains pulled across, they became private cubicles. In the daytime, the travelers sat in luxurious seats. She'd peeked inside and saw the porters letting down the comfortable beds and the stream of women going to the washroom to prepare for sleep. As for her, she had no qualms about sleeping in her padded seat. Getting her son back was a lot more important than a bed.

The train stopped again to take on more coal and water. Jack sauntered down the aisle and joined her. "You didn't pay for a sleeping compartment either?" he asked.

"I'm saving my money. What's your excuse?"

"Haven't you heard?" He winked. "Cowboys don't sleep.

Especially with the rash of train holdups. Don't want them to catch me by surprise."

"Pays to keep one eye open. There was a bad holdup a few months ago when bandits robbed the train out of Winston, Missouri. You might've heard of it. Four people lost their lives, and the robbers got away."

"I read about that. Trains are getting held up all the time, but Frank and Jesse James have moved their sights on to banks, thank goodness. Then there's the Youngers and Daltons." He turned to her. "Has sharing the last name of Dalton made life difficult for you?"

Fancy let out a deep sigh. "If I'm not getting crude comments about my first name, I am my last. People automatically assume I'm kin to the infamous Daltons. But I'm not."

"I never thought you were. What was that you said? Something about coming from honest, hardworking people. I could see that. Would you like to go to the parlor car for a bit?"

"I think I would." She pushed her bag under her seat and led the way to the spacious car where passengers could relax and sank into a cushioned seat.

Two men at a table finished their card game and left in a serious discussion about politics. No one else remained.

"This is better." Jack pulled his chair close to Fancy.

"How is Reno?" she asked, hoping for good news.

"He's no worse. I'll change his bandage tomorrow and see what the gash looks like." He took out some tobacco and rolled a cigarette. "Do you mind?" he asked before lighting it.

"No, go ahead."

She'd long observed that a lot of men had to have something to do with their hands, so smoking was usually what they did. Older men whittled or read. Women liked to occupy themselves knitting or darning. For Fancy, it was watching people. They fascinated her and she loved to imagine their lives.

She and Jack talked about a good many subjects. Fancy told him about her mother and how possibly she'd never see her grave again.

"Why not?" he asked.

"I really have nothing to return to. I sold all my belongings and told my landlord I wouldn't be back. I intend to get a job in Denver in a café or laundry. Once I complete my reason for making the trip, I'll stay. Even if it doesn't work out. The chances of winning are slim."

Jack reached for her hand and looked at it a minute before letting it go. "I wish you'd trust me enough to confide but we hardly know each other so I understand. Settling Uncle Anson's affairs may come to naught as well, but I have a ranch to get back to and fight to keep. Somehow. Someway. People like us don't give up, do we?" He leaned back and stretched his legs in front of him.

"It's not in our nature apparently." She would never stop trying to get Daniel back so the people who had him had better get ready to battle. She wasn't going to go away. Her tears long since exhausted, all that was left was sheer determination.

Her virginity had been ripped from her in the dark of night then her baby.

Stolen.

The word still brought chills. She set her jaw. She wasn't going to be a victim anymore. She'd fight and claw and hold on with the last shred of strength until she got back what was hers.

"When I was younger, I never thought things would be so hard." Jack glanced up. "Kids are in such a hurry to grow up, not realizing that making a good life is a lot of difficult work."

"For sure. Piper will have a rude awakening if she thinks

she can run off and be a Wild West trick rider." Fancy shifted and crossed her legs. "Wish I could warn her."

"She wouldn't listen. Youth is deaf and blind."

They rose and returned to the passenger car. Fancy removed her hat and placed it on top of her bag. Jack kept his on and pulled it low over his eyes. Henry came by with a blanket which she gratefully took.

"Thank you." She gave him a warm smile. "You are such a dear, caring man."

"I enjoy seeing to people's comfort, miss." He went on down the aisle handing out blankets.

She spread the soft wool over her and snuggled into the folds. "Goodnight, Jack."

"Miss Fancy, I do hope you have pleasant dreams."

Fancy yawned. Feeling safe and warm, she let her eyelids close.

Before she knew it, daylight was creeping into the passenger car and folks were beginning to stir.

Then she noticed where she was, and the way her face burned, she knew it must be as red as a rooster's comb. She carefully removed her hand from Jack's neck and herself from his chest, praying he wouldn't wake up.

Please just let him sleep. But, just then, he stirred. *Oh shoot!*

"Good morning, Fancy," came Jack's sleep-roughened voice. "I trust you were comfortable?" He pushed his hat back with a fingertip and looked at her.

"I'm sorry I—" Was what? Laying on him like a brazen hussy? "I didn't mean to—"

"I didn't mind being a pillow. You shared your blanket, so it was little enough." He sat up. "It appears we survived the night." He raised his right arm and rotated it, wincing.

"What's wrong?" She frowned. She wasn't *that* heavy.

"Soreness. I'm not used to riding a horse bareback without reins, and especially not a spirited racehorse."

"Oh. I imagine you're a mass of knotted muscle." Fancy

folded the blanket. "I'm going to the washroom. I'll be back in a minute."

And so, their second day of travel began with a silent vow to avoid sleeping in Jack's arms again. The hours passed pretty much the same as the first day with the exception of herding cows.

The train stopped at every town along the way to take on travelers or let them off, plus there was a need to keep refilling the coal bin and water tank. It was painstakingly slow, and weariness had long taken over her body.

One thought kept her focused. Every mile of track took her ever closer to Daniel.

"Daniel baby," she whispered. "Mama's coming."

Jack clutched a telegram he'd gotten at the last stop, staring at the words.

Big problems at the mine. Cook quit. Miners fighting. Need food and pay or quitting.

It was signed Declan O'Connor. Jack sighed and stuck it in his pocket. He wasn't even there yet and already problems were growing. Well, he could do nothing until he got there. He leaned back in his seat and admired Fancy sitting beside him.

She fascinated him as no woman ever had and the dream of a wife and family began to form. He'd watched his brother with his young wife and the happiness they'd found and wanted the same for himself. The way Jack felt went a lot stronger than want. Desire burned inside ever since Fancy fell asleep on him, the curves of her body pressing against him, the faint scent of some light fragrance circling his head.

And there was more. He saw the way she truly cared for Piper and her commitment to watch out for the motherless girl.

Jack never thought he could ever have his brother's kind of love for himself—until now. Maybe he had a slim chance.

First though, he'd have to break the shell Fancy had placed around her heart. She'd seen trouble and heartache, that much was clear. And what was this mysterious thing that someone had stolen from her? Whatever it was, prompted her to sell her belongings and head West.

On the third day, Henry announced that they'd arrive in Denver by afternoon. Jack finally got Fancy alone in the alcove of the empty parlor car.

"I'm getting nervous now that I'm about there, Jack. I'm unable to still this jittery mess inside me." She clutched her hands, staring out the window at passing trees so tall they seemed to brush the sky and mountains clothed in beauty.

She'd changed into a deep purple dress with the same pretty hat that picked up complementary hues. The feminine beauty of the outfit was her style no way around that fact. He didn't miss the frayed hem though. Not that it took from the dress or mattered in the least. She couldn't help her circumstances any more than he could and made the best of what she had.

"I wish you'd trust me. Tell me what you're facing. Maybe I can help."

"It's true that I desperately need a friend, someone to advise me of the right course to take. If I don't do this right..." She turned to him, her gaze dropping to the gun he wore. "What I'm about to tell you stays between us. Promise?"

"I won't tell a soul." He took her hand and found it ice cold.

As she told him her horrifying story in a voice no louder than a whisper, he saw it unfold in his head. The violent assault, the baby, the midwife—it all took shape.

Now he finally understood.

His heart heavy, he lifted her hand to his mouth and

kissed her fingers. "I don't know how you've kept from going insane. I'll help you do whatever you need to in order to right this injustice. I don't have a lot of money but what I have is yours if you need it." He paused and lowered his voice even more. "If you want to steal your baby back, I'll do that."

"That's just it, Jack. I don't know how to proceed but I think I'd like to try appealing to these people's sense of right and wrong first." She pulled her hand back. "Maybe they're good decent people. In fact, that's my hope. I'll show them the statement Mrs. Winters wrote."

"Excellent plan. That would be my first move." He admired her logic and clear thinking.

"I haven't thought beyond that. What if they refuse? Do I go to the sheriff?"

"I think seeking an attorney might be the wisest thing." He hated to tell her that the midwife's statement really wasn't proof of anything. The event would have to be investigated, and that could take quite a while.

Tears filled her eyes. "I don't have any money for an attorney, Jack. I'll find a job right away, but it'll take time to save up on a waitress's pay." Her lip quivered as she lowered her eyes to her lap. "What if they pack up and leave in the meantime and I never find Daniel again? I just want to see him, hold him, and tell him how much I love him. It's all I think about."

He yearned to comfort her, to take her worry and put a smile on her face.

"I'm so sorry." His voice was gentle. "It doesn't cost any money to speak to an attorney, and maybe he can file something in court preventing these people from leaving Denver." He pushed back a strand of her red hair. "First things first. Appeal to them as a mother and see what happens."

"Of course." She inhaled a deep breath and gave him what

passed for a smile, although it lacked a bit of curve. "Thank you. I feel better just having your support."

"Someone once said burdens are lighter when shared and I believe it to be true." He removed the telegram from his pocket. "I have something bothering me as well. Can I run it by you?"

"I would love to help if I can."

"Okay. I sent a telegram to O'Connor at the last stop and got this in return." He handed her the slip of paper. "I don't know what to do about it. I'll have to see an attorney first myself and change everything over to my brother's and my names before I'll have any authority."

"Yes. As soon as you do, you'll have to ride to the mine and work out something with those miners. Hopefully, you'll have the money to pay them." She tapped her chin with a fingertip. "As far as the food goes, I can cook. At least for a while."

"You know, even a few days will save me and give me time to find someone else. I have to try to keep these miners, or the mine will be worthless. But I wouldn't want to delay your plan to get your baby boy." He rubbed his eyes. "I wish my brother was handling this. He's much better than I am only he has a wife who's in the family way and couldn't leave her."

"You'll do a good job." Fancy's eyes had a mischievous twinkle. "I'm sure your brother wouldn't have been near as competent at herding cows with a racehorse."

"I don't know about that." This easy camaraderie with her sent a warm glow to Jack's heart. And so did the knowledge they'd see each other after they arrived instead of parting ways.

There was something about Fancy that spoke to him, and it went beyond mere talk of problems.

He studied her soft lips and wondered what kissing her would be like. Who knew? But he sure wanted to find out.

"Unless I'm mistaken, Miss Fancy, we've struck a deal. I'll help you get your baby back if you'll cook a few days for me while I smooth the miners' ruffled feathers."

"Agreed. Or as much as I'm able right now." She lifted her chin. "I do plan to see my baby first and speak to the people who have him." Her voice broke and she fought to keep her composure. "I hope you understand how my arms ache to hold him and snuggle his sweet neck." Tears filled her eyes. "I've waited so long."

How he admired this strong pretty woman who gave her all to find the baby she'd birthed. He pulled out a handkerchief and gave it to her.

She dabbed at her tears and gave him a weak smile. "I'm sorry."

"Don't be. I understand."

They both had so much to do upon arrival, but for him, his horse Reno and Piper had to get immediate attention.

Still, a few of the knots in his belly loosened.

CHAPTER SEVEN

That afternoon, the big orange sun hung low in the sky by the time the train whistle blew as the 1216 pulled into the Denver station. Fancy was a bundle of nerves as she prepared to deboard.

Impeccable as ever, Henry approached her. "The stolen bag aside, I trust you enjoyed the trip."

She clasped both his hands. "It was delightful. I'll always remember your kindness."

Henry leaned close, his gaze meeting hers. "Miss Fancy, Coltrain cares for you. I've seen it and so has everyone else. Give him a chance and I think you'll find happiness beyond your wildest dreams."

She glanced at Jack in deep conversation with a man. "We'll see."

"Don't take love lightly, dear, especially if it's the true kind. All I'm asking is that you keep the door open."

"I will, Henry. Thank you for your many kindnesses." She kissed his cheek.

"I speak from recent experience," Henry said. "I've been terribly lonely since my wife passed on but things have changed. I, too, found love here on the train and will be married next week. I've already given my notice to my boss."

"Congratulations! That's wonderful."

"Thank you. I'm going to spend the rest of my days spoiling the new missus." Henry glanced around, his eyes misting. "There's something magical here on this train."

Fancy's attention strayed to Jack a few feet away. "Indeed, there does seem to be."

Wishing each other good fortune, they parted, and she joined Jack on his way to the baggage car. After weaving through the travelers, they stepped inside to collect Jack's bags and help Piper. The girl looked relieved to see them.

"Willie, it looks like we've arrived." Fancy took the baggage man's large, callused hand. "Thank you so much for all you did. I wish you Scruffy well in all your travels. Maybe I'll see you again sometime."

"Miss Fancy, Jack, what you said goes for me too." Willie wiped his eyes. "Friends." He shook their hands then took Scruffy from Piper. "Scruffy and me'll miss you."

Piper threw her arms around the hefty baggageman's waist. "I love you, Mr. Willie."

He nodded, too choked up to reply. Piper sat primly on the coffin to wait.

As the wheels of the powerful train came to a stop, Willie set Scruffy down and slid the wide door open. "Here we are."

Scruffy yipped and jumped around their feet. He finally ran to Piper and she picked the dog up.

Jack collected his bag from Willie and set it next to Fancy's. "Wait here. I'll see if I can find O'Connor and we'll get Piper's mama off."

A few minutes later, he was back with a muscled man driving a wagon. "O'Connor sent this man to get Piper."

The girl stared at the driver, her voice dripping with scorn. "See? I told you my grandparents didn't want me. They couldn't be bothered to come themselves."

"Oh honey." Fancy folded her arms around the girl. It did seem she was right. "Please try not to judge them. Maybe something came up."

"Yeah." Piper snorted. "Something more important than me."

Nothing useful to say came to mind, so Fancy looped her arm around Piper's and walked down a plank to the wagon while Jack and the silent hired man loaded the coffin and baggage. Jack went to get Reno from the stockcar and tied the injured horse to the back of the wagon.

As they drove toward a livery, Fancy stared back at the train and knew her friend Evie had been right. She'd found kind people along the way and made friends she wouldn't forget.

Henry's words sounded in her head. *There's something magical here on this train.*

Yes, there was, and she prayed it continued. Now that she'd finally reached the town that held her son, her insides jumped with anticipation. She wished she could go directly to Daniel and demand him back but instead had to restrain that urge. Acting rashly would ruin her chances. She had to be smart to win.

They left Jack's horse with a capable hostler who would treat the gelding's leg before winding their way through busy Denver streets with buildings taller than she'd ever seen. Trees filled every vacant space adding lush beauty to everything.

At last, they turned into a fancy neighborhood filled with stately two-story houses. Fancy had never seen this many fine homes in one section before. It appeared the O'Connors had money. Maybe they thought Piper had her sights on that or that she was a little thief. No telling what they thought, but any decent grandparent would've met their granddaughter's train.

Her face set in grim lines, the girl was sullen and subdued, almost as if she was going to her death.

"This looks nice, doesn't it, Piper?" Fancy pointed to a cute dog in the yard at one home.

"I miss Scruffy," Piper murmured. "I hope him and Willie will be okay."

"I'm sure they will, honey."

Up front, Jack was getting nowhere in carrying on a conversation with the driver. The man hadn't said three words.

Finally, they turned into a drive and went around to the back of the house. The driver got down and walked toward a little house. A tall, scowling man came out and a tiny woman stood on the top step of a small porch.

"Are you O'Connor?" Jack called to the frowner. "Piper O'Connor's grandfather?"

For a moment, Fancy thought the man wouldn't speak.

Finally, he answered in a curt tone, "I'm O'Connor. Never knew I had a granddaughter."

"He doesn't want me," Piper whispered. "He doesn't."

Fancy put an arm around her shoulders and found them trembling. "Let me help you out. I'm sure when he sees you, he'll change."

Jack jumped down and she and Piper climbed from the back of the wagon. Fancy shook out her skirt then wrapped the girl in her protective arms as they walked forward.

"Mr. O'Connor, I'm Fancy Dalton and this is your… Piper." Fancy stuck out her hand, daring the man to refuse her. He hesitated a moment before accepting the handshake.

Without introducing himself, Jack shook hands next. "We met Piper on the train, and she was in need of a friend."

"How much money is that going to cost me?" O'Connor barked.

The woman on the step appeared to flinch but maybe it

was distance that made Fancy think that. The strange woman still had yet to speak a word.

Fancy drew herself up straight. "Jack and I don't expect or want any payment for simple human kindness. We're decent people who saw Piper's need for someone to care." He could keep his money and stick it inside his rude heart. "All we intend to do is to help Piper bury her mother and make sure the child has a good home."

Jack glared. "Now if you can't do that, we'll take the girl off your hands."

"You'd do us a favor." O'Connor peered at Jack. "You the girl's father?"

"No. I told you we met her on the train. I'm Jack Coltrain of Omaha. I came to meet with Declan O'Connor after he notified me my uncle had died. I don't suppose you're him."

Lord, Fancy hoped not.

"I'm one and the same. I wrote you about Anson. Why didn't you say so?"

Some of O'Connor's rudeness vanished toward Jack, but Fancy saw no such bending for herself and Piper.

"I'll take care of my business with you once we conclude this with Piper." Jack's words held frost and a sharp edge. "Are you going to bury her mother, or will we have to scrape together enough ourselves?"

O'Connor released a heavy sigh. "I don't know why I should, but I'll put my daughter in the ground."

"And what about your granddaughter?" Jack pressed. "Do you intend to do right by her?"

The question was followed by a lengthy silence. Piper fidgeted uneasily.

"Not sure she wants us any more than we want her," the stiff-necked man said, refusing to look at Piper.

"I'm leaving!" Piper yelled. "I wouldn't stay here if you begged me!" She whirled and ran to the wagon, tears running down her face. "I told you! Mama was right."

"Run off! Go ahead." O'Connor waved an arm at her, his anger coloring his face red. "You're exactly like your mother."

The woman by the door began to silently sob. She fumbled for the knob and disappeared inside.

Fancy went to Piper and pulled her close. "I'm so sorry."

Everyone, starting with her own mother, had let the girl down. Fancy murmured soothing words, rubbing the thin spine that had borne such a heavy load.

Behind her, Jack asked for a ride back to the depot. Fancy couldn't wait to be gone. The man was despicable. Whatever happened between Piper's mother and her parents had been bad.

And lasting it appeared.

"Take the wagon but meet us at the cemetery tomorrow morning at nine sharp," O'Connor answered. "I'll put that woman in the ground."

That he couldn't bring himself to even say his daughter's name made Fancy's chest ache. He made no further mention of Piper, never gave the child another glance. Deep sadness filled Fancy as she helped the girl onto the wagon seat.

"I'll also speak to you tomorrow about Uncle Anson." Jack climbed onto the wagon seat. "I want to be done with that because right now I want to knock the whey out of you for your treatment of this sweet little girl who never did you one speck of harm. You might think about that." He lifted the reins and got the horses moving.

O'Connor stood watching until they turned around and went down the drive. The afternoon was swiftly fading, and they had yet to find a place to sleep.

Jack's profile in the growing darkness suggested he was mulling over the conversation with O'Connor. Anger still showed in the tightness around his mouth and the muscle bunching in his jaw.

Other than an occasional sniffle, Piper made no sound. Fancy couldn't imagine what was going through the girl's head, but had a pretty good guess. Being unwanted would send anyone into a dark depression. The urge was strong to go tell O'Connor what she thought of him.

The ill-tempered old goat.

The slight woman on the steps crossed her mind. Maybe approaching her would get better results. But no. O'Connor seemed to have her under his thumb as a good many men these days who never let their wives have a voice. A lot of those same narrow-minded men had frequented the Whistle Stop Café where she'd worked.

"Jack, do you have a plan for tonight?" Fancy asked softly.

"I'll find a place for you and Piper. I can sleep anywhere, even in this wagon. Might be best anyway to discourage brazen thieves." He turned her direction. "If I had the money in my pocket, I'd bury Piper's mother myself and tell O'Connor where to go."

"Me too." Fancy tightened her arm around Piper. "Where is common decency?"

"Not here, that's for sure. Let's get us a bite to eat while we lay out a plan."

"Sounds good, Jack. Piper's probably hungry."

The girl stirred. "Not much. My stomach hurts."

It was nerves. Fancy's was also tied in rigid knots and she didn't dare think about her baby right now. Not with the way things had gone so far. She pointed to a quaint café tucked into a cozy bunch of trees that brought a fairy tale to mind. "Would you like to try there?"

Jack stopped and they went inside. About half the tables were full. They selected one against the wall and sat down.

A smiling waitress approached. "The special is on the blackboard on the wall. I recommend it."

The board had fried chicken with mashed potatoes and green beans.

Jack spoke first. "I'll have the special with coffee."

Fancy and Piper chose beef stew with cornbread. "Milk for us," Fancy added.

When the waitress turned to put the order in, Fancy stopped her. "Excuse me, ma'm. We're new to town and wondering where we might find sleeping accommodations relatively clean and cheap. We're not particular."

The woman named several hotels then lowered her voice. "If you're looking to stay more than a day or two, try Miss Susan's Boardinghouse three streets north. She runs a fine place, and you won't find any riffraff there. Miss Susan is strict about that. I think her rate is $1.25 a week for families and that includes two meals a day." She glanced at Piper. "Your daughter's a pretty thing. She looks tired."

Fancy opened her mouth to tell the woman they weren't a family but changed her mind. "Thank you, ma'am. You've been most helpful. We've been traveling all day and worn out."

After the waitress left, Fancy leaned toward Jack and spoke quietly. "I think I'll take the room at Miss Susan's for Piper and me if there are any vacancies. It sounds nice and private plus we'll get meals. I doubt I can find anything else at this price that is more reputable."

"We'll drive over there when we finish and check it out. I want you somewhere safe."

The protective note in his voice warmed Fancy's heart.

Piper laid her head on the table. She was dead on her feet and heartsore. Poor thing.

Fancy laid a hand on the girl's back. "We'll see how big the room is. You told me cowboys don't sleep, but if the room is large, we might fit you in there too. The floor wouldn't be half bad."

He shook his head. "I'm planning on going up the mountain to Cripple Creek as soon as I can, so don't worry about me. Anywhere is good for a few nights. I just want to get you taken care of."

Why couldn't she have met Jack long ago before her world took a shattering turn? Sudden hotness lurked behind her eyelids. How many men considered her welfare over his? Not very many and none that she knew personally.

She didn't argue and enjoyed her meal when it arrived. Even though she hadn't been that hungry, she ate every bite of her stew. Piper finished about half which was better than she'd thought. She sat back, her stomach happy and glanced at Jack's plate of nothing but chicken bones. He'd been starving, and even after finishing off his meal, still ordered a round of buttermilk pie.

When she tried to help pay, he waved her off. Fancy shook her finger. "We're going to have a serious conversation about our finances."

A hint of a smile brightened his face—the first since meeting O'Connor. His deep voice sent quivers through her. "When I get where I can't afford a meal, Miss Bossy, I'll let you know. Right now, I'm in good shape."

"As soon as I complete our agreement, I'll see about a job." Fancy took a sip of water. "I have to have some income." Money would aid her fight for Daniel. And fight she would. She was his mother, and she was going to claim him. Now, she also had Piper to care for.

"Fancy, I'll pay you for the cooking you do for me. Uncle Anson has to have had a little money to pay his miners. I won't ask you do this for nothing. Does that ease your mind?"

"It does. I hate having the matter of money between us."

"Me too." He covered her hand with his for only a moment but it was long enough to strengthen her.

They left soon after and soon pulled up in front of Miss Susan's.

Fancy clutched his arm. "Jack, isn't this pretty? I feel at home already."

The two-story white house with green trim was

surrounded by tall pines with beautiful flowers spilling from the numerous flowerboxes underneath the windows. A cute little tan and white dog that appeared to be a mixed breed trotted from around the house with tail wagging to welcome them.

Piper jumped down to pet it and laughed when it licked her face.

"Looks like she's found a friend," Jack remarked, helping Fancy down.

"I love the sound of her laughter. Jack, I don't care what O'Connor decides tomorrow, he's not getting her. She'd die there."

Jack took her arm going up the walk. "Forget dying, she wouldn't stay there long enough for that. She'd run off to who knows where and probably starve to death."

He lifted the brass knocker. Piper scampered onto the porch just as the door opened.

A thirtyish, attractive brunette smiled. "May I help you?"

Jack removed his hat. "I sure hope so. We're looking for a room, and the waitress at the café mentioned you might have a vacancy."

"I do. You're welcome to look at it." She held the door wider.

"Thank you, ma'am." Jack put a hand on Fancy's back and they went inside.

Fancy decided to tell the truth up front. She didn't want any lies standing between her and gaining custody of her son. "Just me and the girl will need accommodations."

"That's right. I'll be staying elsewhere," Jack said.

"I like it here," Piper whispered. "But I need to stay with my mama. She'll need me."

Fancy eyed a nearby chair with a needlepoint seat. She sat and pulled Piper onto her lap and smoothed back her hair. "Sweetheart, your mama's in heaven, not out in the wagon.

You need rest to get through tomorrow. Jack will guard her I promise. Please?"

Piper bit her lip. "Are you sure?"

"I'm positive your mama will be safe from harm while you get some rest."

"Okay, I guess."

"Good girl." Fancy kissed her cheek. They got to their feet and joined Jack and the woman.

"By the way, I'm Susan Cready." The woman took a key from her pocket.

Jack introduced them, then Susan led them up the stairs to a room at the back. A pretty quilt covered the bed, picking up the vibrant rose-colored curtains. A dresser, chest of drawers, washstand, and small table completed Fancy's inventory of the furnishings. It was perfect.

Jack met Fancy's gaze, lifting a questioning eyebrow. She gave him a nod.

"Since it's just you and the girl, I can let you have it for a dollar a week plus two meals a day." Susan Cready rested a light hand on Piper's shoulder and smiled.

"I'll take it." Fancy took a dollar from her pocket. "Can we move in tonight? We just arrived in town and have nowhere else to go."

"Of course, my dear."

"What's your dog's name?" Piper asked.

"Taffy. She never meets a stranger." Susan laughed. "I often wonder what she'd do if confronted by a burglar. Probably lick him to death."

"I like her. She's cute and Taffy's a good name." Piper went down the stairs.

Fancy's gaze followed her. Thank goodness she appeared happier. "I'm not Piper's mother, Miss Susan. Her mother died, and we're burying her in the morning. Piper's been very distraught so I'm happy to see Taffy put her in better spirits."

"I'm so sorry. She's far too young to deal with death."

Or life either, especially this one. Fancy inhaled a deep breath. This was good. She liked it here. The rooms were light and airy and there seemed no better landlord than Susan Cready. Yes, they'd get along well.

Hopefully, the house, the dog, and Susan were good omens.

Fancy blinked back sudden tears, wishing she could tell her mother. But she'd have even more happy news when she got Daniel back.

Her baby was so close she could almost reach out and touch him.

CHAPTER EIGHT

Jack carried the women's bags up to their room. "You ladies sleep well. I'll see you in the morning." Clutching his hat that had seen better days, he went out into the hall.

Worry darkened Fancy's eyes as she stepped outside the room with him. She'd removed her pretty hat and light from an oil lamp on a small table in the hallway illuminated the soft lines of her face, bringing out the deep brown of her eyes and gold in her copper hair. She chewed her lip. "I hate to see you go. This is a big town. How will I find you in case I—rather we—should need you?"

"I'll be close." He set his Stetson on the small table and faced her, lifting a loose strand of silky hair. He hated goodbyes. It seemed he'd known her all her life.

Why was it that some strangers he met felt like old friends?

Except at the moment, friends didn't describe the feelings tumbling around inside him like a pebble in a stream rushing toward something larger. Fancy had crawled into his heart. She reached for his hand, gripping it.

"In fact, if you step out the door here, I'll see you and

come running. How's that?" With a gentle touch, he tugged her a little closer, feeling the wild beating of her heart.

"Then you must have decided to sleep in the wagon." She didn't look happy about that either.

"It's best to keep the curious away. A loaded gun in the face will convince them of the error of their ways." Jack squeezed her hand. "Try to get some sleep. We'll have decisions to make tomorrow."

"You're right. But I'm not going to let O'Connor be mean to that little girl in there. If I have to take her to raise, I will." The stubborn angle of her chin said she meant business.

"Don't forget, I'll be right there beside you." He smoothed a wrinkle on her forehead with the pad of a thumb. "Fancy, we're two of a kind. Two warriors ready to fight the world." He fell into her beautiful brown eyes and his words came out hoarse. "I want to kiss you."

With a quick breath, Fancy stared into his eyes. "I have no objection," she whispered.

His hand drifted up her slender throat to rest under her jaw and he lowered his head. A quiver danced up his spine as his lips touched hers. The initial lightness turned into something more urgent. A faint sweetness of the pie they'd had lingered on her tongue as she leaned into him, returning the kiss.

Now he understood the longing he'd sometimes seen etched on his brother's face when he looked at his wife.

Marriage was an equal partnership and it seemed pretty close to his and Fancy's blossoming relationship. The way they stood side by side during these trials confirmed that. Could he be falling in love? Did love happen this fast?

Though reluctant, he ended the kiss, staring at Fancy in wonder. She was everything he wanted in a wife but had despaired of ever finding. Until now.

She stood, her fingers to her lips. "I'm not sure what just happened, and I have so little experience to know, but does kissing always leave a person feeling like they've been struck by lightning?"

Jack didn't answer for several heartbeats, just stared at her. "No, this isn't normal. I think it's only when you care about someone."

She cupped his jaw and asked quietly. "Do you care for me, Jack?"

"I'd be lying if I said no. I was just thinking that it feels like I've known you forever. I want to smooth the rough spots and help you get your baby back." He took a deep breath. "I care."

"My mother always used to tell me that there's a mate for everyone, and you simply have to find the right person. But I never believed that there was anyone for me."

"Never despair, pretty lady. I should let you get some rest." He reached for his hat and adjusted it on his head. "I'll see you in the morning. Miss Cready said I could come to breakfast." He touched his lips to her soft cheek, hating to leave. "Goodnight."

He turned and strode to the stairs, knowing he couldn't look back. If he did, wild horses wouldn't be able to budge him.

Longing gripped him with each excruciating step that took him farther away from her.

Fancy fell asleep with her arm around Piper and was still in the same position when dawn broke. Jack's kiss still lingered on her lips. It was everything she'd imagined. Also lingering was the tingle she'd felt when her lips had touched Jack's. Oh, to kiss him again! To be held in his strong arms and shielded from life's problems.

Was it so wrong to want that?

Piper's eyes fluttered and she rubbed the sleep from them.

"How did you sleep, sweetheart?" Fancy asked softly.

"Good." The girl stretched. "I dreamed of Mama, and she told me not to be afraid. She said she'd always be with me. But I can't help being scared. I don't know what's gonna happen. I can't go live with that horrible man. I won't."

"I agree. Do you have any other kin at all? An aunt or uncle?"

"Mama didn't mention anyone. It was always us two." Piper sat up. "She was an only child and never spoke of any other family."

Fancy undid the girl's braid. "Do you know who your father is?" she asked gently.

"Mama said he died. That's all I know."

Who knew if that was true? It could've been a convenient story.

"Okay. Here's the deal. You'll stay with me. Will that be all right?"

Hope filled Piper's eyes. "Can I?"

"I dare anyone to try to take you. I'll fight with all the strength I have."

"I'm glad you want me."

"Sweetheart, I love you, and that's what people do when they love someone. They care for them and keep them safe." She tweaked Piper's nose. "Let's get ready for breakfast. I want to get down there and see how Jack spent the night. He's eating with us."

"Good. I really like Mr. Coltrain. He's nice and doesn't treat me like a kid." Piper stretched. "He stood up to mean ol' Mr. O'Connor too. Did you see that?"

"I certainly did." Fancy had been praying hard that Jack wouldn't hit the man and he'd come mighty close. She threw back the covers. "This is a very comfortable bed. Don't you think, Piper?"

"The best. Mama's and mine had lumps and a hole in the ticking that let goose quills pop out and stick me."

The more Piper talked of her life with her mama, the more desperate their situation sounded. Their home probably wasn't more than a hovel at best.

"My bed wasn't nearly this good either." Fancy slipped on a clean dress then combed her hair and twisted it in a low knot on the back of her neck.

Piper sprang into action. "A dress for Mama's funeral." She smoothed the skirt. "Do you think she'll be scared being underneath the dirt? It's real dark down there."

"No, honey. Your mama is safe up in heaven. Only her body is in that coffin. It's like a caterpillar that leaves a shell behind when it changes into a butterfly. Your mama is a beautiful butterfly flitting all over heaven, not feeling any pain or worry."

"I'm glad. She didn't like the dark." With a sudden sobbing cry, Piper threw her arms around Fancy's neck. "I miss her so bad. I need her. Why does it hurt so much?"

"Because your heart is broken. It takes time to heal and to fill the hole our loved ones leave." Fancy washed away the girl's tears and braided her hair then they went downstairs.

Jack was just arriving. His eyes lit up. "My girls look mighty pretty today."

"Thank you. You look nice too, Jack." Fancy tried not to blush like a schoolgirl but was sure she did. Thank goodness Piper took over the conversation and asked a million questions, saving Fancy from having to pry.

"I slept with one eye open," Jack said with a grin. "Kept my finger on my gun, ready to shoot anyone if they tried to bother your mama." He rested a hand on the girl's shoulder. "I kept watch like I promised. Did you have any bad dreams?"

"Nope. Just a good one. I dreamed of Mama and she told me that she'd always be with me. Do you think she will, Mr. Coltrain?"

"Absolutely. I'm sure of it."

Four boarders besides them filled the table and introduced themselves. One was a schoolteacher, one a clerk in the mercantile, another worked in the bank, and the last one at the newspaper. They were all very friendly. Fancy was sparing with details about her life saying only that she was starting over after the death of her mother. She offered little about Piper as well. Jack told them nothing more than that he was going up the mountain to Cripple Creek.

The meal was simple but divine and they thanked Miss Susan. Fancy told her she couldn't help clean up the dishes but would another time and promised to help with other meals.

Miss Susan waved them on. "I understand. Don't give it a thought."

The pretty woman who worked at the newspaper, Nessa, spoke up. "Miss Fancy, I've offered to help. You folks go on. I have a little time before I head to the office."

Fancy thanked her and donned her hat and gloves before hurrying out. The day promised to be sunny with a few fluffy clouds drifting lazily overhead. Piper sat somber between Jack and her, hands tightly clasped. The dress she'd donned was worn, but pretty, and made her look like a young woman. Fancy knew the girl's uncertain future crowded her mind. It was on hers as well. She and Jack spoke in low tones, remarking on the beauty around them. The trees were so tall, they appeared to touch the heavens and the crisp air was the freshest she'd ever breathed.

She'd noticed how quickly she ran out of breath with the least exertion and had overheard talk on the train that the effect of the high altitude would cause this. She hoped she got used to it soon.

Jack flicked the reins. "When this is over, I'll have to go check on Reno's condition."

"Yes, we should find out about his injury," Fancy agreed, fingering the scrap of paper in her pocket with trembling fingers. "Then will you take me to the house where Daniel lives? I can't wait another minute. I have to see him."

"I promise." Jack's smile deepened the lines at the corners of his eyes. "I'll offer to rent this wagon from O'Connor. If he refuses, we'll be afoot."

"Maybe the old goat will relent. It's not like we're asking for it for weeks. Only a day or two." The slight breeze ruffling a feather on Fancy's pretty hat, she put an arm around Piper seated between them. The girl rested her head against Fancy's shoulder.

"If he refuses, I'll walk to the nearest livery and rent transportation." Jack turned into the cemetery.

It took no time to find the O'Connors waiting in a handsome buggy. Two gravediggers rested on their shovels at an open hole. Jack backed the wagon as close as he could so they wouldn't have to carry the coffin far.

Piper began to weep in great, gulping sobs. Jack lifted her down and she buried her face in his shirt. Fancy already had tears welling up as well. She murmured soothing words. While Jack and the other men unloaded the coffin, she took Piper's hand, and led her toward the stiff-necked O'Connors

When they reached the grandparents, Fancy nodded. "Thank you for coming."

Neither of them responded, but she thought the woman's quiet words to her husband sounded tearful. Or maybe that was only because Fancy willed the woman to show some bit of emotion. Surely, they both felt something, some morsel of regret or sadness for their daughter.

Piper clung to Fancy, burying her face in Fancy's shoulder.

Another buggy arrived and a minister got out. The grandparents must've arranged for him and it shocked Fancy that they had. Perhaps they did have some caring deep down for their daughter.

Fancy shook the minister's hand and thanked him for coming.

"May I speak with the girl for a moment?" the young man of God asked. His kind eyes and soft voice assured that she could trust him to not upset Piper further.

"Yes, of course. Any comfort will be welcome." Fancy relinquished her hold.

The minister took Piper's hand and they stepped away from the group.

Fancy took advantage of Piper's absence and approached the grandparents. "Thank you for arranging the minister. That was nice."

"Our daughter spurned God. My wife and I prayed for her soul," Mr. O'Connor said tightly. "We thought Piper might appreciate a proper burial though."

A glance at Piper and the minister found the girl shaking her head at something he said.

"Mrs. O'Connor, I didn't meet you yesterday. I'm Fancy Dalton. Your husband probably explained that Jack Coltrain and I met Piper on the train and immediately felt obliged to see to her welfare until she is with family." Fancy paused for a heartbeat to give the woman time to speak. When she didn't, Fancy went on. "I'm sure it's a shock to have a granddaughter you didn't know existed show up and you need time to adjust to her. Jack and I think it's best to keep Piper with us for a little while. She also needs some space to adjust to you as well."

Frankly, Declan O'Connor appeared relieved and began to relax.

"Thank you, Miss Dalton." The missus glanced toward Piper. The woman wore a thick black veil that prevented Fancy from seeing her eyes. "It's not that we don't want her exactly. Our reluctance—"

Declan put a rough hand on his wife's arm and shook his head, shutting her up. "When our daughter left Denver, she never looked back or gave us another thought. She left trouble everywhere she went, and she'd disrespected us for the last time. I packed her things and drove her to the train depot and told her never to darken our doors again. I did it for her own good."

Their daughter's good? That was a joke. They'd done it for their own sakes and nothing more.

"We agree that Piper should stay with you and we're grateful you're keeping her," Declan said. "Maybe in time we'll feel differently. I don't know."

Jack joined them, sliding an arm around Fancy. "I couldn't help overhearing your conversation. Our concern is that little girl over there who's lost and alone. I have to say that I'm appalled by your seemingly cold attitudes. But your loss is our gain. We love Piper and will take her to raise and ensure her happiness until you make up your minds."

CHAPTER NINE

A fierce need to protect Piper rose up, the intensity almost strangling Jack. Mr. O'Connor glared following Jack's statement and the missus began to cry. Jack didn't know exactly how Fancy felt about adopting Piper, but he had a pretty good guess. In the short time he'd known her, he'd seen her deep commitment and love for this little girl who needed a secure home. A secure life.

"Look here," O'Connor blustered. "Threats will get you nowhere. Give us time to figure this out. Besides, no judge will grant adoption to you since you're unwed." He paused and narrowed his eyes. "I gather that's the case since you have different last names."

The man was right. They weren't wed, but Jack could remedy that in a heartbeat and was ready to do so.

"Please, let's take a deep breath." Fancy turned to Jack. "You know where I stand on this and I'm ready to marry you if that's what it takes. But let's not rob the O'Connors and take away their chance to make a decision. Still, I won't put Piper's happiness in jeopardy either." She faced the grandparents. "We won't drag this out indefinitely. Let's set a time limit—say two weeks."

Declan's eyes shifted to Piper and the minister. There was a hint of something there.

"I think that's reasonable," Jack agreed with a nod. "How about you, O'Connor?"

For once, Mrs. O'Connor straightened her spine and put steel in her voice. "It's more than fair. I can see how much Piper loved her mother and is shattered at losing her. None of the past is her fault. She's just a kid, Declan. And she has our blood in her. We can work this out."

"I agree," Jack said, breathing easier at the man's nod.

Piper returned with the minister and seemed comforted by whatever the man of the cloth had talked to her about. She stood between Jack and Fancy, clutching their hands. The service was beautiful there under the pines with a gentle, fragrant breeze rustling through the branches. The angels seemed to be singing and the birds added happy tweets, flitting overhead.

At the end of the heartfelt words, the minister reached into a large box for a birdcage with a white dove inside and turned to Piper. "Let's release your mother from this life and give her peace."

Tears rolled down Piper's cheeks as she opened the door of the cage that the minister held. A smile formed. "I'll always love you, Mama. Fly away to heaven and rest. The preacher says I'll see you again one day. Oh, how I love you."

The dove emerged and flew skyward. A fitting tribute for her mother's sad life.

The minister shook hands all around and hugged Piper. "Remember what I said. Your mother is safely with Jesus and walking on streets of gold."

Piper nodded. "I like that. Mama loved glittery things. She'll be happy."

As soon as the preacher left, Jack spoke low, "Fancy, keep Piper company while I have a word with O'Connor." He approached the man he had business with and cleared his throat. "Can I have a word, sir?"

The man nodded and they stepped away for privacy. Jack met O'Connor's gaze. The man was hard, but Jack wouldn't let that intimidate him. "First, thank you for the loan of the wagon. I really appreciated that. Now I want to ask if you'll let me rent it for a few days. We're afoot."

"No," O'Connor answered. "You can't rent it."

The stinging words slapped Jack's face. "I have good money and will pay up front. If your answer is still no, will you take me to a livery where I can rent one?"

"No." Then O'Connor smiled. "I'll loan it to you."

Jack felt like hauling off and slugging the man for making him think the worst. "Thank you, sir. Like I said, it'll only be a few days. I have legal matters to settle then I'm going up to Cripple Creek."

"I'd hurry if I were you."

"I plan to." Jack glanced down at O'Connor's fancy boots then at his scuffed ones that probably still had a bit of manure on the bottoms. "Sir, can you explain your relationship with my uncle?"

"I was a friend." Oddly, the lines in O'Connor's face softened. "I own the mine next to his, and we whiled away the hours playing poker and talking. I found him slumped over a table in his shack. He'd once told me if anything happened to him to contact you. I did."

"Thanks." Jack studied the man through narrowed eyes. "So, the mine is producing?"

"Like a motherlode. The only thing is his crew of six are threatening to walk off. They haven't been paid and the cook quit, so they're having to scrounge for food. I took some supplies up to get them by, but you need to take more. And a cook. And pay them for current and back wages before they cart off whatever gold they can carry. The foreman has his hands full."

Jack glanced at Fancy. "I already have a temporary cook. I'll head there as soon as I can."

O'Connor pushed his hat back. "Cripple Creek is just starting to amount to something, but I guarantee that once the news of gold gets out, it'll become a boom-town overnight." He paused. "There are dangerous greedy people lurking around who would as soon kill you and dance on your grave."

The warning raised the hair on the back of Jack's neck. "Was Uncle Anson murdered?"

"No, that was a heart attack. I'm saying be careful and be prepared to fight. They'll take the mine from you in a heartbeat if you show any sign of weakness."

"Understood. I don't think they'll find me an easy target."

Dangerous people weren't anything new. Jack and his brother had fought for all they were worth to hang on to their land and buried a few hard learners who kept coming after them.

"Thank you, O'Connor." Jack shook his hand. "We have a lot of business to take care of and need to get started. I appreciate the use of the wagon."

O'Connor stared at Piper. "My granddaughter is a pretty little thing."

"Yes, sir, she is." Jack strolled toward the women wondering what in the heck to make of the man's odd statement.

Moments later, they settled in the wagon, and he drove to the livery.

"I'll only be a few minutes." Jack met Fancy's gaze and drowned in her beautiful brown eyes that held misery and plenty of nervous anticipation. He had to take her to her baby as soon as possible. The delay was wearing on her. "I promise."

She managed a half-smile. "I know you're doing your best."

He glanced at Piper asleep on the seat with her head on Fancy's shoulder. The kid was worn out. Grieving sapped a person's energy. Sleep would do her good. He sighed and went inside the structure.

The hefty hostler came from a stall with a black bag. "Coltrain, ain't it?"

"That's right. I came to check on my horse."

"Good news. The cut wasn't as deep as I thought and missed the tendons." The man scratched his balding head. "Give him two weeks and he'll be as good as new. I'll keep doctoring him, and he should be fine."

Relief flooded through Jack. "I can't thank you enough. Reno means a lot to me and to lose him would be devastating."

The man nodded. "He's a fine animal."

They shook hands and Jack returned to the wagon. "Reno will be fine," he announced.

"Oh, that's wonderful!" Fancy's smile lifted the shadow that had hung over the day. "I'm so happy for you. I could see how worried you were."

He settled on the wagon seat and lifted the reins. "I was mighty worried. Now, what was that address?" Jack met her guarded expression. She wanted to be hopeful but was afraid. "Our good luck has to carry over."

Fancy nodded, silently handing him the paper Mrs. Winters had given her.

After stopping twice to ask directions, they finally turned into a beautiful neighborhood. The houses weren't half as elaborate as O'Connor's but nice all the same. Each home had a new coat of whitewash and white picket fences across the front. Trees and colorful flowers grew in abundance. It looked like a great place in which to grow up.

"What do you want to do?" He reached across Piper and took Fancy's icy hand.

"I think I should go alone this first time." She squeezed his fingers. "Jack, I'm so scared. Now that I'm here at last, I don't know what to do or say."

Jack could understand that. The best thing would be not to show anger, but she might be unable to keep from it. Her flesh and blood had been stolen, ripped from her arms.

"Fancy, just remember that these people didn't conspire to hurt you. True, they knew it was wrong, but who knows what Mrs. Winters told them. Maybe she let them think you'd died. Direct any anger to the poor excuse for a midwife." He dropped her hand and brushed her soft cheek with a fingertip. "Are you sure you don't want me to go with you?"

"Thank you, but this is something I need to do alone."

Piper stirred as Fancy got out. Jack's gaze followed her up the walk. He put an arm around Piper and said a silent prayer.

Fancy took deep breaths as she stood before the door, patting a strand of hair into place beneath her hat, praying she looked her best. All the what-ifs ran through her head. This was the moment she'd yearned for since starting out. Her hands shook and her knock wasn't loud enough. She started to rap again when the door opened.

A pale, dark-haired woman smiled, but it carried no warmth. "May I help you?" She looked to be only a couple of years older than herself. She coughed into a lacy handkerchief, and Fancy took note of her thin body. Clearly, she wasn't in the best of health.

A little boy, tugged at the woman's skirts. The breath lodged in Fancy's throat. For a moment, she couldn't breathe.

Daniel. It had to be.

He wore the sweetest shy grin that melted her heart. Mischief lodged in his eyes, the brightest, clearest blue she'd ever seen. She yearned to reach for him.

"Miss? May I help you?" the woman repeated.

Don't show anger, Fancy told herself. "Mrs. Bishop?"

"Yes?"

"I'd like to speak to you about a personal matter of great importance."

"I'm a little busy. And I have no need of whatever is it you're selling."

Fancy clutched her hands tightly. "I'm selling nothing, ma'am. I've traveled a long distance." She wet her lips. "It's about your child."

"Come in." Madeline Bishop opened the door wider, and Fancy stepped inside.

Sunlight spilled through the large windows, giving the house an outdoor feel. But Fancy's attention riveted on the child. Her child.

The toddler silently held some blocks out to her.

Tears welled up, but somehow, she kept them from falling. "Hello, darling. You are such a handsome little man." She touched his tawny hair and found it silky just as she'd imagined.

Coughing again, Mrs. Bishop directed her into the parlor. "Have a seat, miss. As I said, I haven't much time."

The two-and-a- half-year-old played quietly with a pull toy on a beautiful Persian rug.

Fancy fumbled for the paper Mrs. Judith Winters had given her and clasped it between trembling fingers. "My name is Fancy Dalton, and I came from a small town outside Omaha, Nebraska." Fancy inhaled deeply and blurted, "I believe you have my child."

CHAPTER TEN

"No!" Madeline Bishop screeched, color draining from her pale face. "You're mistaken." Her lips thinned even more. "Daniel is mine. I don't know what you're trying to pull, but it won't work. Is this some scheme to get money out of us?"

"Money is the last thing in the world I want, ma'am. Please hear me out. I beg you."

She couldn't get kicked out before she could reason with the woman. Just then, the toddler climbed into Fancy's lap with two colorful building blocks. Her heart leaped with joy to hold him at last. The weight of his small body filled her with a rush of overwhelming happiness as she kissed his soft cheek. He touched her face. Such a sweet baby fragrance swirled around her. She soaked it all up.

Madeline jumped to her feet and snatched Daniel. "How absolutely shameful to come in here and make such appalling accusations. Are you accusing my husband and I of stealing your child? Is that your intention?"

"No, ma'am. I'm accusing the woman who gave Daniel to you. I have a note here written by someone I believe you may know or had business dealings with—Judith Winters. She gave me your address. Please read it." Fancy held out the paper. "Please just take a moment."

The irate woman stared at the note as though it were a snake about to strike. Color drained from her face as she finally took it and scanned the words. "This proves nothing. Daniel is ours! My husband will deal with you. He's an attorney and a good one. Get out!"

Fancy kept her voice gentle. "You had to have known it was wrong when you accepted him. Unless... Did Mrs. Winters lie to you as well? Maybe she told you I died in childbirth. Was that the case?" she asked.

"I...we..." Mrs. Bishop stuttered, then anger took hold. "Get out! Now!"

The order shut down any further conversation before Fancy could get any answers.

"You can find me at Miss Susan's boardinghouse. I'm not going away until I get this sorted out." She walked to the door. "If Daniel is truly yours, can you provide anything to prove it? I'm a reasonable woman and would never take a child from its mother."

Anger flooded Madeline Bishop's face, and her lips curled. "I'm his mother!"

"I'm truly sorry. I can see your love for Daniel, and I had hoped to appeal to you mother to mother. Although I never got a chance to hold him or kiss his cheek, not a day has gone by that I haven't...loved him..." Fancy's voice broke. For a moment, she struggled to compose herself. "Not a day that I haven't grieved for him. Help right this wrong that's causing us both such wrenching agony."

Through blinding tears, Fancy opened the door and stumbled into the bright sunshine but felt none of its warmth.

Jack was waiting just outside, seeming to know she needed him. He put an arm around her waist to support her. "It'll get better. We have to trust that it will."

"I don't know, Jack. She's so livid."

"Don't give up. That'll help nothing."

His deep voice provided comfort and strength at the same time. He helped her into the wagon and got her settled before going around. The wagon rocked with his weight as he got in.

Piper folded Fancy in an awkward embrace. "Miss Fancy, don't cry." The girl patted her back. "I don't want you to be sad. If that mean ol' lady hurt you, I'll go kick her in the shins."

The picture brought a smile. Fancy took a handkerchief Jack pressed in her hands. She dried her eyes and blew her nose. "I'm fine, Piper. I'm sorry to upset you on such a sorrowful day of your own."

Through the throbbing pain in her chest, she clung to practicality. "Jack, I need to speak to a lawyer right away. This may get ugly."

"I agree that's best. Since I need to see the lawyer handling my uncle's affairs anyway, we'll ask him."

As he set the wagon in motion, she told him all that had happened, then gave him a watery smile. "I got to hold Daniel for a moment. I can't tell you the joy that flooded over me to feel his little body and kiss his cheek." A sob rose with the remembrance and the fact she had to leave him behind. "He's such a handsome boy. So sweet."

"Who's Daniel?" Piper asked in a small voice. "Why did he make you sad?"

Here was the question Fancy knew she'd have to answer. "Daniel is my baby boy. I lost him and now I've found him again. Only, the people don't want to give him back."

Piper frowned. "So now that you found your baby, does that mean you don't want me?"

"No, no, no, honey." Fancy took Piper's hands in hers. "You're under our care and it's going to stay that way. Nothing or no one will change that. Understand?"

"I think so." Piper's frown vanished. "I'm glad. But it made you so sad to see him."

"That's because I had to leave him with the Bishops. For now, at least."

"I love you, Miss Fancy. Can I call you Mama Two? Like the number two. Can I?"

The question stunned her. Fancy exchanged a glance with Jack and he nodded.

"I think this means a lot to Piper." His voice had roughened and sounded rusty.

"Honey, you are welcome to call me anything your heart desires." Fancy pulled her into her lap and kissed her cheek. "I sort of like being Mama Two. It has a nice ring to it."

"I'm glad." Piper rested her head against Fancy's chest and gave a happy sigh.

Jack had to again ask directions and finally pulled up in front of a brick building with the name Townsend Kilpatrick, Esquire emblazoned across the front. With a name like that, he had to be smart. Fancy prayed he was at least smart enough to get Daniel back.

She glanced at Jack, curious why he hadn't moved. He'd never looked more handsome, broad-chested, and strong with dark, wavy hair beneath the black Stetson. It thrilled her to be seen with him. He scanned the street for several heartbeats, his gray eyes taking in every detail. The Colt he wore at his hip added a hint of danger about him, although he'd never frightened her.

"What?" he asked, shifting on the seat.

"I was just thinking how happy I am that our paths crossed. It had to have been fate." She took a deep breath. "Ready?"

They climbed out and with Piper between them, went inside. Jack removed his hat and requested to see Mr. Kilpatrick.

A woman at a desk smiled and led them into an office. "Wait here."

They hadn't waited but a few minutes when the door

opened and a tall, distinguished gentleman with graying hair and a closely-cropped beard bustled in. Townsend Kilpatrick shook hands and introduced himself then took a pair of spectacles from an inside pocket of his pin-striped suit and slipped them on.

Clutching his hat in his hands, Jack introduced himself. "I believe you're handling my uncle Anson Beckett's affairs."

"Ah, yes. I wondered when I might expect you."

"I caught the first train coming this way. He owned a mine up at Cripple Creek." Jack filled him in on the details. "My brother, sisters, and I are the next of kin."

Townsend Kilpatrick went to the door and spoke to his secretary. She wasted no time in bringing Anson Beckett's file. "Let me see." He rifled through the papers, scanning them and raised his head. A smile formed. "Mr. Coltrain, do you know how much your uncle was worth?"

"I really can't hazard a guess, sir. Uncle Anson kept his affairs to himself." Jack glanced at Fancy and shrugged.

What was the lawyer trying to say? Had Jack come all this way for nothing?

Piper tapped Fancy's shoulder. "Mama Two, what's going on?" she whispered.

"I'm not sure yet." She thought Mr. Kilpatrick had a nice smile. Older women probably thought him attractive—herself included.

"How does two hundred and fifty thousand dollars each sound?" Kilpatrick asked.

Jack thrust his hands through his hair. "Are you sure we're talking about the right man? I haven't seen Uncle Anson lately, but he never had two pennies to his name."

"I'm positive. His mine finally started to pay off." Kilpatrick leaned back and crossed his ankles. "Anson Beckett was a crusty man and never joked much. But he always believed he was going to strike it rich. I was sorry to hear he'd passed. I'll miss the curmudgeon."

Miss his money most likely. Fancy plucked at a piece of lint on her dress. How was this going to affect her relationship with Jack? Money changed people. She was as poor as the church mouse. He'd probably want a fancier, different kind of woman.

Piper tapped her again. "Is Jack rich?"

"Yes, it does seem so." Fancy studied the face of the cowboy she'd become so familiar with over the last several days. Her mother would've liked him. She and the old Jack would've been friends. But Fancy wasn't sure about this new one.

The pact they'd made crossed her mind. He wouldn't be interested in helping her get her baby back now.

Kilpatrick hollered to his secretary to bring some papers then turned to Jack. "As soon as you sign the proper forms, you'll become the new owner of the Beckett Mine."

"I still can't believe it. My brother and I had hoped Uncle Anson would leave a few dollars but nothing like this." He grinned at Fancy. "We can afford to fight for your baby now."

He hadn't forgotten their pact. Her heart leaped.

While they waited on the secretary to bring the papers, Jack had Fancy tell Kilpatrick about her stolen baby.

When she finished, she said, "Please tell me what to do and how to proceed. Every second away from my child is pure agony."

Kilpatrick laced his fingers and put them behind his head. "The bond between a mother and her child is the strongest power on earth. But love has formed between your son and the Bishops by now. To take the boy from them at this stage could cause severe trauma." He blew out a big breath. "This won't be easy to resolve. Someone is going to suffer, Miss Dalton. Are you prepared to lose?"

Fancy faced him, blinking back tears. "There hasn't been a day I've forgotten about his birth. I've sorely grieved for the child I grew inside me. I talked to him, sang, made plans for our life together. I loved him then, Mr. Kilpatrick, and I love him now. This has taken a huge toll on me. As big a one as the Bishops should they lose this fight. I don't harbor any ill will toward them, but they surely knew taking Daniel as theirs was wrong."

"Would the violent way in which the baby was conceived have any bearing?" Jack asked.

"I'm sorry for what you suffered, Miss Dalton. Was the man caught?"

"No." Fancy looked down at her hands as memories swirled of that dark night and the figure leaping from the alley. The hand over her mouth, the smell of whiskey that made her gag. His bruising grip that had brought cries. "If ever anyone deserves to go to hell, it's that animal."

Piper pressed close and patted her arm. "It's okay, Mama Two."

"I know, honey. Thank you." Fancy kissed her cheek, grateful for the child.

Jack went to the window and stared down on the street below. "I had planned to go to Cripple Creek tomorrow. Uncle Anson's friend told me about trouble with the miners that I need to straighten out and hire a new cook. Miss Fancy's agreed to fill in until I find one, but we can postpone that if need be."

Townsend Kilpatrick leaned forward. "Miss Dalton, I think the best way to proceed is to give me some time to check everything out. While I do, think about going on to Cripple Creek and cook for Coltrain. Badgering the Bishops will only make them dig their heels in deeper."

"I think that's sound advice." Jack swung to Fancy. "How soon can you be ready?"

"Say the word and I'll climb in a wagon or on a horse." She wanted to say more, but it wasn't the right time—if there was one. Who knew when something was right? She'd always trusted a gut feeling and let that be her guide.

The secretary came in with the papers and, with a few strokes of a pen, the ownership of the Beckett Mine transferred to Jack.

"That does it." Kilpatrick scribbled a note and handed it to Jack. "Take this to the First National Bank on Seventeenth Street and you'll have full access to Anson Beckett's account."

Jack stuck the paper in his pocket. "Thank you, sir. You've been most helpful." He put a hand on Piper's shoulder. "We have one more piece of business before we leave."

He told the lawyer about the O'Connor's unwillingness to take their granddaughter. "Fancy and I are prepared to raise the child. If it comes to that, how do we make it permanent?"

Piper sat up, listening to every word.

Kilpatrick frowned. "Do you think O'Connor will challenge you and take her?"

Jack twirled his hat between his hands. "We don't know. But we need this settled."

"I don't want them, and they don't want me," Piper stated, her chin raised to a defiant angle. "I want to stay with Mama Fancy and Jack."

"We only want the best for Piper, sir. Her happiness means everything." Fancy's soft words filled the room. "She's been through so much in her short life. She deserves to be a kid—a happy one."

"I see." Kilpatrick laid a hand on Piper's shoulder. "Then we'll try to do that. If the grandparents raise no objections, it'll be fairly simple. Let me see what I can do while you're up in Cripple Creek. I can make you her guardians, but I need to check into something first." He jotted in a notebook then raised his head. "I don't know how you feel about it, but marrying might be the only way you can get Daniel and keep Piper."

CHAPTER ELEVEN

"We'll consider your advice." Jack thanked Townsend Kilpatrick for his time, and they left.

Out on the street, Fancy filled her lungs with the fresh mountain air. "The worry and fears that sat on my shoulders are gone, Jack. I think we found another warrior."

"Kilpatrick seems very capable." Once Jack helped her and Piper into the wagon, he stared at the law office. "I feel like I'm dreaming, and this will all be gone when I wake up. My head is spinning."

"Mine too. This money will change your life. It'll save your ranch, Jack."

"Thank you for bringing that up. I need to let my brother know." He turned the wagon toward the telegraph perching between a doctor's office and mercantile.

"Then can we eat?" Piper asked. She pointed to a café next to a tall hotel. "That looks nice. How about it, Mama Two?"

Fancy nodded. "It's perfect. I don't think any of us ate much breakfast."

"I like it here." Piper swiveled this way and that, trying to see everything. "I think Mama's happy."

"I'll bet she's smiling." Jack maneuvered the wagon around some riders who'd stopped. He wondered if Fancy had heard Kilpatrick's statement about marrying. She hadn't batted an eye. The unfortunate thing was they couldn't talk about it in front of Piper.

Maybe when they got back to the boardinghouse, the girl could play with the dog and give them a minute.

As for him, he'd tie the knot any time the pretty lady agreed. He loved the jaunty angle of the hat she wore. It fit her. The soft curve of her cheek and determined jaw, her becoming hair style, and the sweep of her long lashes set his blood humming. Heat curled along his spine at the thought of sharing a life with this courageous woman who'd stolen his heart with her kindness and gentle ways.

But what did she think of him? Would she find him lacking? They hadn't had time for a slow, easy relationship.

So busy admiring her and thinking about marriage, Jack let his attention wander.

"Watch out!" Fancy cried.

Jack swerved hard to avoid a collision with a child chasing a ball. "Surely his mother teaches the boy about playing in the street."

"He's young."

"Well, he won't stay alive much longer if he keeps doing that." Scolding himself for daydreaming, Jack kept his eyes glued straight ahead and pulled up in front of the telegraph office. "I'll only be a moment."

"Take your time. Piper and I are fine," Fancy assured him.

He went inside, and with a shaking hand, soon got the telegraph sent telling his brother the Denver bank would wire the money to pay off the ranch. Jack could picture him when he got the message and the relief and joy on his face. They'd struggled hard for so long, and now it seemed things were finally beginning to work out, thanks to Uncle Anson.

The truth was starting to sink in—they were well off.

He'd need some money for the trip up to Cripple Creek but wondered how much. To him, a hundred was a whole lot, but probably pennies to a person of wealth. He'd need to buy extra supplies, pay the miners what he owed them, and maybe make a few repairs. Plus, he and Fancy needed money to live on. He pondered it all before he went back to the wagon. He'd take out a thousand. If he needed it, he'd have it. If not, he could deposit it back in.

His mind made up, he joined Fancy and Piper and aimed the wagon toward Seventeenth Street. The bank was an imposing three-story brick building.

Jack stopped the wagon and pulled the brake. "I'll be right back and take my two favorite girls to eat at the best restaurant in Denver."

"I hope we look okay," Fancy fretted.

He gave her a long look. She might not be wearing expensive clothes or jewels, but she rivaled any woman in the city. "You're beautiful. Both of you. I'm a lucky man."

Winking at them, he hurried inside and presented the note from Townsend Kilpatrick. A clerk led him into a private office and handed Kilpatrick's note to a man at an ornate desk. The nameplate identified him as the bank president.

The man wore a grin that suddenly stretched from ear to ear. He stood. "Have a seat Mr. Coltrain. I'm Walter West, and it's a privilege to take care of you."

"Thank you, Mr. West." Jack shook hands and sat down.

"An imported cigar?" The man extended an open box.

"No, thank you."

"One of our calendars?"

"I suppose." Maybe Uncle Anson's cabin would need one. Jack took it, laying it in front of him. "Sir, I appreciate the warm welcome, but all I'm here for is to withdraw some money. A thousand should do it."

"Of course. Let me speak to the clerk, and you can walk

out with it. How do you want it? Large bills, small? And do you have anything to put the cash in?"

Good Lord! He hadn't thought about any of that. He had a feeling he'd never know how to act like a rich man when poor was all he'd known.

With a mixture of large and small bills, he left the bank with the cash in a fancy leather bag. Mr. West explained he kept a stash of the bags for his most important customers. Jack dared anyone to try to take his. They'd have the fight of their lives.

Over a late meal that afternoon in the Minton Hotel, he and Fancy made plans to leave for Cripple Creek the next morning. The sooner they got up there, the sooner they could soothe the miners and concentrate on getting Daniel back. But for now, they were following Kilpatrick's advice to let the lawyer work his charm on the Bishops.

Jack glanced at Fancy, happy to see she was eating more than a few bites. Piper too. He didn't want them getting any skinnier. "I need to buy my own wagon and team then take this one back to O'Connor. I don't like feeling beholden to the sour man."

She nodded. "I agree. I would feel better. So we'll buy the new wagon and I'll follow you over to the O'Connors."

Piper played with her food. "Mr. Jack, I don't know what to call you. Mister doesn't sound right. Fancy is Mama Two, but I never had a papa before. And I'm going to be staying with you and Mama Two."

"What do you want to call me?" he asked quietly. "I can be anything you feel comfortable with."

"How about Daddy Jack?"

Daddy. The word struck the most vulnerable, secret place deep inside him like a bass piano key. He'd never been one. Not even close. But the sound of it thrilled him. He glanced at Fancy and she smiled.

He took Piper's hands in his. "I think I'd like that, honey. I'd like that a lot."

"Good." The worry on Piper's face vanished with her grin. "Now that that's settled, can we go visit Mama's grave for a minute? I want to tell her something."

"Of course." With everything they had to do, he didn't know how he'd spare the time, but he would for a sweet girl who asked for so little. "Now, who would like dessert? I saw ice cream on the menu."

Piper's hand shot up first, then Fancy's.

Fancy's soft brown eyes danced. "Jack Coltrain, you are bound and determined to make me fat."

"Wouldn't make any difference to me," he replied. "I'll take you however you are." And he meant that. He wondered what she'd say to an idea that had settled in his brain. He propped his elbows on the table and stared at the way the light from the chandeliers created a halo around her. So beautiful. "I doubt you've ever been fat a day in your life."

"Well, I might start."

Piper was staring at them, probably wondering what their conversation meant. Thank goodness the ice cream came and took her attention.

As soon as Fancy finished the last bite, Jack laid his napkin down and asked for the check. "Let's get out of here."

They went back to the livery and spoke to the hostler. The man only had one. "It's new so it'll cost you, Coltrain."

"That's fine," Jack said agreeably. "How much?"

"Sixty-five dollars. For a pair of horses, it'll be another $150."

Jack counted out the money and Fancy climbed up on the seat. Piper scrambled up and they went back to the O'Connor's. Not seeing anyone, they left his wagon with a note and took Piper to the cemetery. The day had been a long one.

It was late and the sun hung low in the sky when they

arrived at the gravesite. The girl sat next to the mound of dirt and let some sift through her fingers. Fancy and Jack stood by the wagon, giving her time to speak her thoughts, although they couldn't help overhearing.

"Mama, I hope you're happy up there on those streets of gold. I miss you something awful." A curious little bird hopped close by, and Piper stared at it. "Please don't be mad at me, but I asked Miss Fancy to be my mama and Mr. Jack, my daddy. I love them so. They're going to take care of me until I can come up there with you. They're real nice and Miss Fancy is pretty like you. Mr. Jack owns a gold mine now and I don't exactly know what that is but maybe that means he don't hafta worry about money anymore. But me and Mama Two are still poor. Mr. Jack might give us money if we need it though 'cause he's nice."

Jack glanced at Fancy and his hand stole to hers and squeezed. "Isn't our girl something? I will share all I have with you both," he whispered.

Behind them, Piper went on with the talk to her mother.

Fancy's eyes met his. "What are you saying, Jack?"

"Wait until we have some privacy. There's a lot I want to say. And do more of this." He leaned to kiss her. Her breath was soft and fragrant as it mingled with his.

He'd just deepened the kiss when Piper stood and dusted off her hands. "Well, that's all, Mama. I just wanted to tell you what's been happening. Oh, I forgot to tell you that Mama Two has a little boy but mean ol' people won't let her have him on account of they're stingy. She says that I'll still be her girl though and has enough love for us both. Bye for now, Mama."

The feel of Fancy's lips on his left a roar in Jack's ears as wild horses stampeded through him. Sweat lined his palms. Good grief! You'd think he'd never kissed a woman before.

He stepped back from Fancy and turned to Piper. "All finished, honey?"

Piper smiled. "For now, but I'll have more to say next time."

"I'm sure you will, sweetheart," Fancy said, blinking rapidly, her face flushed.

From the looks of it, she was as flustered as Jack was by the kiss.

Still appearing a bit shaken, Fancy avoided his gaze when they climbed in the new wagon pulled by a pair of matching black horses to head for supplies.

"It's all right, Fancy," he said low. "I couldn't resist."

"What, Daddy Jack?" Piper asked.

He noted the becoming shade of Fancy's flushed cheeks, wishing he was a painter. "Something between Mama Two and me, Piper."

Thinking it best to move on, he gave the reins a shake and soon reached the center of town, turning onto the main street. "For once, it seems very odd to get everything we need and not have to worry about how to pay for it. This is definitely going to take some getting used to."

"Yes, I'm sure it will." Fancy strained to look at a pretty blue dress in the window of a shop.

Jack took note of where it was. He yearned to dress her in beautiful clothes.

That night, while Piper chattered up a storm with Miss Susan and the other boarders, Jack took Fancy for a walk.

Butterflies flitted in his stomach. There was no way to predict how Fancy would react.

The sun had just slipped beyond the horizon as they strolled along a garden path behind the boardinghouse. A profusion of spring flowers scented the mountain air.

Fancy slipped her hand in the crook of Jack's elbow. "I can't get over how beautiful it is here. I love it. The peace has been good for my soul. Piper's too, I think. The cool air seems to carry a healing power." She inhaled deeply. "I still have this sadness that goes all the way to the bone but it doesn't consume me like before."

"I've noticed that too." Jack cast her a side glance. There was just enough light left to see every detail of her arresting features—and sadness that lined her face. "What's wrong?"

"My roots are scattered, Jack. Torn and scattered to the breeze. I've always had the comfort of deep roots. I hate this feeling of not belonging somewhere." Tears swam in her brown eyes. "Can you..." She bit her lip. "Can you hold me?"

"Come here." He opened his arms and she walked into them. "Don't be afraid," he murmured into her hair. "The unknown is scary, but you'll put down deep roots again when you find a new home. You'll know when it happens. You have to cling to faith and believe."

She laid her head on his shoulder. "I've never been brave enough."

"I totally disagree with that, lady. Look at what you've faced alone. I marvel at your strength. Your courage." He rubbed the proud lines of her back, soaking up the feel of her in his arms. It felt right. Her heart's rhythm beat softly against his chest.

Finally, she stepped away. "Thank you."

"Better?"

"I am." She gave him a little smile as though to prove it.

They strolled until they came to a bridge spanning a creek and stepped onto it. Fancy leaned against the rail beside him, staring down at the rushing water. "I've always marveled at the unseen force that keeps creeks and rivers in their banks, taking the water on to its destination," she noted quietly. "Sometimes I feel that same force guiding me to something bigger. Something larger. A place where I'm meant to be." She turned to him. "What? Why are you looking at me like that?"

"How can I help it? Your beauty is the kind that stops men in their tracks. You have the prettiest eyes that reflect your sweet, loving spirit." He found trouble swallowing and brushed a silky tendril of hair from her face. "Actually, it's odd that you mention the same thing I want to talk about. Bigger, grander plans that fit together like pieces of a puzzle. Water and puzzle pieces are the same and go where they're meant to be creating something grand."

"I love that," she murmured breathlessly. "You're a deep thinker, Jack Coltrain."

She turned back to the picturesque creek her thoughts unreadable. In the soft twilight, her slender neck seemed perfectly sculpted, and her upswept hairdo further completed the picture. Little wisps of red-gold hair curled on the canvas of her pale skin.

Trembling, he lowered his head to kiss the sensitive skin of her neck and nuzzle behind one shell-like ear.

She slowly swiveled, her gaze searching his eyes. "Jack," she whispered, placing a hand on the side of his face.

He gulped a mouthful of air, hoping it would settle his nerves. "I've been pondering how to say what's in my heart, and I guess the only way is just to blurt it out." He lowered to one knee. "Will you marry me, Fancy Dalton?"

CHAPTER TWELVE

Fancy's heart pounded. Marry him? In truth, she'd gone out of her way to avoid matrimony because the institution appeared nothing but a chain and left wives in horrible shape if their husbands turned out to be abusive or, heaven forbid, died.

The slight breeze lifted a lock of Jack's dark hair and she wanted to touch it. How could she not take a chance of throwing her lot in with his? She trusted and liked him.

But was that enough?

She finally, found her tongue. "Jack, we haven't known each other but a short while and it feels like we're rushing this. I always thought people married for love." She took a tremulous breath. "Do you love me?"

He kissed her fingers. "People marry for all sorts of reasons, and I suspect a good many don't find love until they settle into a life together. I care for you very deeply and you're the kind of woman I always hoped to find. Piper needs us, and being married will also help you regain custody of your son."

"That is true. But can you be a father so suddenly to

someone else's children? Can we talk about this?" Fancy pulled him to his feet.

"Yes, to both questions. How do you feel about me?" he asked softly.

She met his honest gaze. "I was drawn to you when we met on the platform of the train station. Your smile makes my knees weak."

Jack grinned. "I do that?"

"Yes, but don't get a swelled head. Your hat won't fit."

"Ha! Very funny."

"The thing that really makes my heart turn flips is how kind you are to Piper. I know that's not an act. You are truly honorable, compassionate, and caring. You didn't have to open up and let that child in, but you did. And I love that about you. I never knew men like you existed."

Especially after the horrible experience that left her broken. She'd been slow to trust men since, unsure of their motives. But Jack was different.

"She's a sweet kid, and I know your Daniel is too." Jack kissed the sensitive flesh of her wrist. "I will have no problem being a father to them. Being blood kin means little to me. If you agree to be my wife, I will love and protect them always, no matter what comes." He paused, seeming unsure how to put something. Finally, he appeared to take the bull by the horns. "Fancy, I won't ask you to share my bed. When and if you decide to, it'll be your decision."

Relief washed through her. "Thank you, Jack. I don't think I can right now."

"There's no rush. I'm not going anywhere."

Fancy inhaled the heady fragrant air. "Being married *will* remove some of the roadblocks, but when will we do it?"

"To be clear, are you saying yes?"

"I'm ready to take a chance, Jack. I will be your wife, to have and to hold."

He gave a whoop, picked her up, and swung her around. "You sure know how to make a man sweat."

"When will we do this?" She clutched the railing when he set her down. Was this lightheaded feeling the result of his ear-splitting smile or the altitude? Maybe a little of both.

"Tomorrow before we head up the mountain? Wearing my ring could ward off unwelcome suitors. But we can wait until we come back down if you'd rather."

Fancy cocked her head to the side and studied him. "Tomorrow might be best."

"You don't know what a happy, very proud man you've made me." He took her face between his hands and tenderly kissed her.

Tears lurked behind Fancy's eyelids. How she wished her mother could be at the ceremony. She was starting this new scary and exciting journey alone. She clung to this man who'd blazed his way into her life and stolen her breath. Marriage was what two people made it and Fancy would give it her all.

Maybe somewhere along the way, love would blossom. And it would be magnificent.

That night, Fancy relaxed in the boardinghouse parlor talking with Miss Susan and Nessa, the newspaperwoman. She'd shared her plans to marry Jack come morning and they were discussing the ceremony. Jack had left to get a room for the night and Piper was in the kitchen with Taffy.

Someone rapped at the front door and Miss Susan went to answer. She came back with a visitor. "Mrs. Bishop would like to speak to you, Fancy."

Fancy glanced up in surprise. "Mrs. Bishop, of course we can talk. Won't you have a seat?"

The other women made excuses and quickly left. Fancy

couldn't imagine what Madeline Bishop had on her mind to seek her out.

"Has something happened to Daniel?"

Madeline smoothed her skirt and clasped her hands. "No, he's fine. When I thought of the way our conversation went and how rude I was, I had to come apologize. It's just that I hadn't expected you to show up on my doorstep. Now that you're here, I don't quite know what to do."

"I don't mean you any harm, but I'm prepared to do whatever I must to get my child. I think I deserve a chance to know my son and give him all the love that's in my heart."

The woman began to cough and fumbled in her beaded bag for a handkerchief. Fancy pulled one from her pocket and handed it to the woman.

It was several moments before Madeline could speak. Fancy didn't miss the blood on the linen. "Thank you for the handkerchief." Madeline wadded it in her hand. "I fear I've ruined it. I'll take it home to wash."

Fancy touched her arm. "Mrs. Bishop, are you ill?"

Madeline lifted her chin, her features proud and a little haughty. "It's none of your concern. I'm fine." She pulled her arm from Fancy.

How odd of the woman to make light of the blood? If she were ill, what would Daniel do without the woman he'd known as Mama? "I doubt that. I think you are." There was nothing to be gained by arguing, however. "Why are you here? Both of us love Daniel and want the best for him. Can we not be reasonable? I want to tell you how he was conceived."

Fancy spoke of the attack and how the aftermath devastated her. "I wallowed in so much guilt and shame, but then I realized I'd done nothing to cause it. Something precious was stolen from me that night in the hard dirt of that alley, something I could never get back."

The memories swirled as Fancy rose and paced across the

floor. "When I found myself pregnant, everything changed. I had this light inside me that rooted out the darkness. I was so happy to have such wonderful love replacing the evil. For nine months, I talked to the baby and sang. I made plans for the life we'd have. But he was stolen from me." She whirled. "Do you know what it's like to have your child stolen and be told he died? I think you haven't a clue."

Madeline's face became a mask of stone. "Judith Winters is my sister. That's what I came to tell you. I have my own heartbreaking story, so spare me yours."

The shocking statement filled the quiet in the little parlor and sent Fancy reeling.

"Judith Winters is your sister?"

"Yes. She'd helped me through four miscarriages and knew how badly my husband and I wanted a child. We lived in Omaha then and Judith was my only hope. She never planned to steal Daniel. It was a spur of the moment decision. I was there in the house that morning and had just suffered another devastating loss. But Judith walked in with Daniel, and suddenly everything was all right."

"But he was mine!" Fancy shook from head to toe that the woman still felt justified.

"Judith had learned of your circumstances and knew you couldn't afford to give Daniel the life my husband and I could."

"So you judged me! In a few precious moments, you and your husband weighed Daniel's chances and found me wanting!" Fancy trembled with rage. She shook a finger. "Shame on you! Shame...on...the both of you! I would've worked my fingers to the bone to take care of all his needs. I still will if given the chance. I paid dearly, suffered so that he might be born."

Her face livid, Madeline jumped to her feet. "I rocked and sang to him. I sat by his bed when he was sick. Took care of him. When he had nightmares, I was the one soothing his fears. You have no right to say I didn't earn his love! I'm a good mother!"

Fancy pinched the bridge of her nose. None of this was doing any good. She cleared her throat and sat down, speaking in a quiet tone. "Mrs. Bishop, I have hired the attorney, Townsend Kilpatrick, and intend to fight to get Daniel back. I've wasted so much time believing the lie that my baby had died. So do what you need to do because I'm not going anywhere. Or giving up."

Madeline jerked her bag onto her arm. "If you think a judge will award Daniel to a poor single mother, you're sadly mistaken."

"I won't be single long, Mrs. Bishop. I'm getting married tomorrow and he has plenty of money." Fancy should've been ashamed for throwing that into the woman's face, but she had it coming. "Mr. Kilpatrick also plans to have your sister arrested. Depending on the part you played, perhaps you also. Unless you have anything else to threaten me with, I can show you to the door."

Her face drained of color, Madeline silently rose and stalked toward the door, coughing.

Fancy followed close behind. "I really would see a doctor about whatever is ailing you."

Madeline Bishop turned and for a moment it seemed she would speak. However, she remained quietly defiant, turned, and disappeared into the night.

Miss Susan must've heard the door and appeared from the kitchen. "I heard your conversation, dear. I didn't mean to, but you were both raising your voices. How can she defend taking your child? That's horrible."

"If the stakes are high enough, people will justify anything." Fancy wearily turned toward the stairs. "I have a wedding to prepare for. The only thing suitable is the rose dress I traveled in, but it's soiled."

"It'll be perfect." Susan smiled. "Give it to me, and I'll take care of it."

"I couldn't ask that of you. You've been an angel."

"You're not asking. I volunteered. Now, go get it." She pointed to the stairs.

Giving up, Fancy went to fetch it. Piper was lying on the bed reading a book Miss Susan had given her. She glanced up. "Have you ever read Aladdin?"

"I sure did and loved it." Fancy pulled out the dress and folded it over her arm.

Piper flipped over. "Do you think magic carpets really exist?"

"Honey, that's a part of the author's imagination. It's not real."

"I know, but wouldn't it be nice if people could travel on them?"

Unsure where this was going, Fancy sat down beside her. "Yes, it would be amazing. Why all the interest?"

"If Daddy Jack could buy one, I'd fly up to heaven to see my mama." Piper's voice sounded so wistful.

"I wish you could." Fancy gave her a hug. "If they were real, I'd buy you one."

"I know." A tear slid down Piper's cheek, and she brushed it away with her arm. "Do I get to do something in the wedding tomorrow, Mama Two?"

"You sure can. We're family." Fancy tweaked the girl's pert nose. "You get to carry a beautiful bouquet of wildflowers."

"I'll hold them real tight! Thank you for letting me be your family."

"I would be real sad if you weren't." A lump clogging her throat, Fancy rose and went to the door then turned. Piper was staring up at the ceiling. Maybe trying to see all the way to heaven.

If it worked, maybe she'd try it too. Fancy desperately

needed her own mother's strength and assurance that she was doing the right thing.

It felt wrong to marry without love even if it was for the right reasons—like she was betraying herself. Still, she'd do anything for Piper and Daniel.

That was the bottom line. She'd put her needs last for their sakes.

And maybe Jack could be right about love following. Faith, Fancy reminded herself. The size of a mustard seed, but so powerful. She had to leave everything to faith and trust it would turn out.

CHAPTER THIRTEEN

Her wedding day arrived before she could blink. The morning was beautiful with high puffy clouds in a pale blue sky. With Denver sitting in a valley, high mountains rose up around the city. Snow covered some of the peaks and sparkled like diamonds in the sunlight. The sight took her breath.

A tap came at the door. Miss Susan must've heard her moving around. "It's ready, dear."

Fancy opened the door and took the garment from her. "Thank you. You had to have been as tired as I was. I thought about everything Madeline Bishop said so I didn't sleep well. That holier-than-thou attitude makes me so furious."

"She hasn't won. You'll get your baby back, and she'll have to live with what she's done."

Piper sat up rubbing her eyes. "I smell bacon. Did I miss breakfast?"

"No, honey. I wouldn't let that happen." Fancy laid the pretty dress at the end of the bed. "But you need to get up now and get ready. We have lots to do."

"Oh yes!" Piper's eyes widened. "The wedding. I forgot."

The speed in which she threw back the cover and leaped out of bed brought Miss Susan's laughter.

The woman excused herself and left. Piper again chose the outfit she'd worn to her mother's funeral and pulled it over her head. They really had to do some shopping, but it would have to wait until they returned from Cripple Creek. They all needed new clothes and underwear now that they had some money. Yet, she still had an odd feeling about using what wasn't hers. Jack's uncle had bequeathed that to him.

Fancy decided she wouldn't use any more than absolutely necessary. Maybe the feeling would pass at some point, but she doubted that. Putting that vexing problem aside for now, she turned her attention to hers and Piper's hair. In no time, they were ready, and she gave the room a long look before she closed the door, thankful Miss Susan would hold it for their return.

"Please, God, let this be the right thing to do," she whispered.

Jack stood at the bottom of the stairs looking quite resplendent in a dark frock coat and trousers. Nothing fancy and no vest, but very nice. A wide smile that showed his teeth stole her breath, and she almost stumbled on one of the steps.

"Ladies, you're looking very beautiful."

"Mama Two really is, Daddy Jack." Piper ran down ahead to hug him.

When Fancy reached the bottom, she took the elbow he gallantly offered. "Thank you."

Taffy charged, jumping up on Piper before they'd taken three steps. They left her to pet the dog and went on.

"I was afraid you'd back out," Jack whispered.

"Thought about it. But here I am." She stopped to face him. "Jack, Mrs. Bishop called on me here last night and admitted that she knew Daniel had been taken from me. And get this—the midwife who found me on the street is her sister."

"What?" Shock crossed his face.

"Judith Winters and Madeline are sisters. Madeline was in the house that day suffering another miscarriage." She told him all the details of their conversation, ending with, "I asked her to leave. I couldn't help it. I was furious."

"I can see why, and I don't blame you."

"Maybe I tipped my hand a little too much. I told her we'd hired Mr. Kilpatrick."

"No, I think that was good. They know we're serious and aren't going away."

"I'm glad you don't think it was a costly mistake."

Jack put an arm around her waist. "Nothing you do will make me think that."

They turned at the sound of footsteps as the rest of the boarders came downstairs.

"Let's go eat. We'll finish this later." Jack put his mouth to her ear. "We have a lot to do after I make you Mrs. Coltrain."

The married name brought sobering reality to the forefront of Fancy's thoughts.

In no time, she stood in Reverend Copeland's parlor with Jack clasping her hand. The reverend's wife sat at a piano playing softly. She was as round as he was skinny. Fancy's knees shook, and again prayed she wasn't making a mistake.

At the end of the short ceremony, the reverend closed his Bible. "You may seal your vows now."

Jack gave her a light kiss, and Piper handed over the bouquet of wildflowers they'd picked.

"We're a family now." Piper beamed. "No one can take me away from you."

"That's right." Wearing solemn features, Jack glanced at Fancy and put an arm around her. "We're a family."

Fancy hugged the child. "You're ours until you decide you

want different. You know, at some point, you might want to go live with your grandparents."

"I never will." Piper wore a look of confidence.

"I've found it doesn't pay to ever say never because that's how sure I'll have to eat my words," Fancy said, conscious of Jack's warm hand on her waist. "Let's go by Miss Susan's to change clothes and get on the road. We need to find your mine."

"Yes, ma'am, Mrs. Coltrain." Jack's sinful grin made her stomach quicken.

Within the hour they began the journey to Cripple Creek. The distance would force them to camp overnight.

When they reached the outskirts of Denver and started climbing, Fancy looked back. She hated leaving Daniel once more. Unshed tears filled her eyes. "I'll be back to get you, my precious." At least she knew where he was. For now at least.

Jack stopped the horses. "Fancy, you don't have to go with me. You can stay here."

"No, I made a pact and I mean to hold up my end. I'm a woman of my word." She pushed back a fluttering tendril of hair. "Besides, it's best to give this a little time. I trust Kilpatrick."

"If you're sure."

"I am. Let's get moving. We have a long way to go."

As the journey became boring, Piper got out and walked, giving Fancy the privacy needed to talk to her new husband.

"I know very little about you, Jack. Do your parents still live?"

"When they got too old and crippled to run the ranch, they gave it to my brother and I and moved into Omaha to live with my oldest sister, and she takes care of them."

"That's good, and it relieves your mind."

"My brother and I are thankful. Joanne was a bratty sister growing up and gave me and my brother a hard time, but she turned out all right." He grinned at her. "We like to say her husband tamed the wild temper out of her."

Fancy laughed. "I'm sure she disagrees."

"Of course."

"How many of there were you?" Fancy shooed a wasp.

"Four. I have a younger sister who's an angel."

"You must've had a very noisy household. I've always regretted not having a sibling. It was just me and my mother."

"What happened to your father?" Jack asked.

"He was a soldier at Fort Kearny when I was little. He rode out with the troops one morning and met his fate. They were attacked and he was killed. My mother and I moved to Omaha." Fancy was silent a moment. The only sound was the clop of horse's hooves and the jingling of the harness. "Sometimes I can still hear my father's laughter. He had this voice that boomed and filled my ears. It wasn't fair that he was taken so young."

"Life's not fair, Fancy. If it were, Piper would still have not only her mother but a father as well."

"True." Fancy watched the girl, again in the trousers and shirt she'd worn on the train, one suspender twisted. "I'm going to make sure she always has people around who care about her. If not us, then someone."

"Don't write off the O'Connors yet," Jack warned. "I noticed a slight sign of thawing."

"I should hope so. That little girl needs her own kin."

Jack reached and pulled her closer. "But until then, I guess we'll do, Mrs. Coltrain."

Fancy swallowed hard. "I don't feel any different." Wasn't a woman supposed to feel something?

"Me either." Jack released her hand to guide the team around some saplings. "That'll probably come later I reckon."

Horrible doubts strangled Fancy. What was she thinking? Only one thing had been on her mind—getting Daniel back.

She'd seen the kindness of Jack's heart, but she didn't really know him. Maybe he was adept at covering his true self.

She'd never trusted any man, so why now?

What would stop Jack from dumping her and vanishing once she held up her end of the bargain and he'd gotten what he'd wanted? Perhaps he meant to leave her stranded somewhere with Piper and take off. Her mouth went dry.

He had money, lots of money. Men with money could easily erase marriage records or get an annulment.

What did she have? A carpetbag full of belongings that were worth nothing to anyone but her. That was it.

"What's wrong, Fancy?" Jack stared at her. "You look like you're about to throw up."

"Nothing. Just thinking about things."

"Like what? You look worried."

She gazed at the trees and beautiful landscape and checked to see if Piper hadn't gotten too far ahead. She looked anywhere but at Jack.

"What's got you upset?" he asked again.

The silence between them stretched. She knew she had to say something. "Our marriage for one, I guess." She decided it was time for a little honesty. "Thinking about the enormity of living with someone I don't know." She turned to face him. "What if you don't like me or find me different from what you thought? What if you change your mind?"

Jack laughed. "Forget that. I know the kind of person you are. I've watched you in action, both on the train and in Denver. You're just having a case of nerves. Some people get cold feet before marrying, but, in your case, you're getting them afterward. We're going to be just fine." He stretched out his leg and winked. "In fact, I predict we're going to be splendid."

"Splendid?"

"Yep." He winked. "You hide and watch."

Just then Piper came screaming from a thick grove of

pines, her face white. "Bear! Bear!" She was running as fast as her legs could carry her. "Help!"

Sure enough, a huge brown bear clambered out of the woods. Fancy screamed as Jack jerked up the new rifle he'd bought with the supplies.

"Hurry, Piper! Oh, Jack, it's going to get her! Do something."

He leaped from the wagon and started running directly for the deadly animal. Fancy's mouth dried, her heart pounding.

What was he doing? Had he lost his mind? The bear would kill him with one swat of a gigantic paw.

Piper was gasping for air by the time she reached safety. Fancy grabbed her arm and helped her inside the wagon, then turned to watch Jack. He was all that stood between them and that wild animal. *Why didn't he shoot?*

Five feet from the animal, Jack planted his feet and raised both arms, swinging the rifle. He let out the most fearsome yells, waving his arms and using the rifle as a club. The bear raised on its hindlegs, baring sharp teeth.

"Get out of here! Go!" Jack yelled. "Get!"

In what looked like confusion, the bear lowered to the ground and stared.

"Get!" Jack yelled again.

Then miraculously, the beast lumbered back toward the woods, and Fancy could breathe again. Jack didn't move until the animal disappeared into the trees.

When he returned, Fancy looked for scratches or cuts on his face but found none. "Why didn't you shoot?" she asked.

"A bullet wouldn't have stopped it and I was afraid I'd miss anyway, and it would get you. Bears are frightened by loud voices." Jack returned the rifle to its place next to him. "My brother taught me to plant myself and yell as loud as I could, so that's what I did."

"You gave me a heart attack." Fancy punched his arm. "That thing could've killed you."

"You're brave, Daddy Jack." Piper looked around. "I thought it had me."

"Well, it didn't. We all got a good scare. Believe me, my legs were shaking like jelly." Jack removed his hat and wiped his forehead with the sleeve of his shirt.

"No one told me there are bears here," Piper accused, frowning.

"There are lots of animals, snakes and all kinds of critters up here." Jack picked up the reins and the team of horses started moving.

Fancy wiped Piper's face. "You're going to have to be careful. Jack's right. There are things here we can't possibly know about."

"I'm staying with you. No more exploring," she said, beginning to calm down. "It was so big and rose up on its hind legs. It was way taller than Daddy Jack."

"It's over now. If you want to walk some, just stay near the wagon." Jack gave her a gentle pat. "There's a good-sized creek on the map, and I think we're about there. We need to let the horses drink and rest a spell. They must be exhausted pulling this load up the mountain."

"That'll be nice. We can stretch our legs and take a breather." Fancy reached behind the seat for a basket of food Miss Susan had insisted they bring. "We can have a picnic."

Piper grinned. "I saw her sneak in a whole apple pie."

"Well, I'll be! That cinches the deal. A picnic we'll have." Jack's laughter seemed to spring from his broad chest like a bubbling, underground mountain stream.

Fancy loved the sound of it. And the wide smile that touched his grayish eyes and turned them to blue-tinted smoke. "Faith," she whispered to herself.

She had to cling to that and keep an open heart. Something she'd once heard her mother say when times were bleak came to mind. "Fancy, life is a journey. Not one trip, but hundreds. We have to keep going and proceed with courage each and every day as long as we have breath."

The memory brought comfort. Jack's hand rested on the seat, and she covered it with her palm, giving his fingers a little squeeze.

CHAPTER FOURTEEN

"Are there any bears here, Daddy Jack?" As they stopped, Piper gave the thick trees around the fast-moving stream a nervous glance.

"No. I don't see any. Want to ride?"

When she nodded, he lifted her up and sat her on his shoulders.

Piper put her arms around his neck. "I see real far now, and no bears can get me."

Jack was almost certain it was safe to say this was her first time on anyone's shoulders. He winked at Fancy who was spreading a quilt on the thick grass and walked down to the water with his passenger. "Can you see any critters from up there?"

"Nope."

Although he needed to help Fancy, he knew how important it was to Piper to feel special, so keeping her up there, he grabbed the lines of the horses, leading them to the water. Then he took the child over to the quilt and set her on her feet.

"That was fun, Daddy Jack." Piper giggled and plopped down on the quilt. "What else did Miss Susan send?"

"There's some left-over fried chicken from last night's supper, pickles, and a half a loaf of fresh bread. I haven't reached the bottom yet." Fancy laughed and the sound was music to Jack's ears. "By the looks of things, she must've thought we were going to starve."

He stretched out on one edge of the quilt and put his hands behind his head, staring up at the sky. "I don't think I've ever seen such a beautiful place."

Fancy followed his gaze upward. "I heard Miss Susan say it's God's country."

"Sounds about right. There's a good plot of ground over there to the north that would be perfect for a house."

"A house?" Fancy gave him a startled glance, handing him a piece of chicken. "Are you thinking of building here?"

"Just voicing thoughts." Jack sat up and took a glass of lemonade. "I really don't know what I want to do. It's all so new and to tell the truth, my head is still spinning. But I'll talk over any plans with you and we'll make them together."

Piper took a chicken leg and wandered down to the water's edge, in plain view of them.

Jack still kept his voice low. "Our marriage is a partnership, and we'll share equally."

"Your uncle left that money to you, Jack. It's yours." Fancy's warm hand on his arm spoke of caring.

A thrill raced through him. His wife was caring and sensitive and he found that knowledge seeping into his bones.

"No, honey. What's mine is yours from now on. We share everything fifty-fifty."

She grinned. "Are we arguing?"

"I don't think so." He softly brushed her cheek with a finger. "It's called discussing."

"Oh?" She moved the picnic basket and leaned over.

A little stretch helped him meet her enticing lips. The kiss was light and quick since Piper wasn't that far away. But it was enough to whet his appetite. He couldn't wait until they stopped for the night and Piper went to sleep. Then he could hold Fancy and feel her soft heartbeat.

"Look what I found, Mama Two!" Piper came skipping back and brought a tadpole for Fancy to admire. Jack had to say Fancy showed proper excitement for the find, although she clearly hated touching the slick creature.

The welcome break in the trip over, Jack packed everything up and set off again.

That night, they camped beside another swift moving mountain stream and huddled near the fire. Now that the altitude was higher, the air was colder. Jack shot some game and Fancy cooked it to perfection.

Come bedtime, Fancy made a bed for Piper and gave Jack raised eyebrows. "It seems we misjudged the bedding situation. We don't have enough blankets."

He took her aside and spoke quietly. "Did I not mention that we share equally?"

"Yes, but—"

"Can you sleep at my side and trust me not to touch you? Can you do that this once?"

Her eyes widened in the light from the campfire. "Sleep with you?"

"I know I promised you'd have your own bed, but due to unforeseen circumstances, can you set that aside for this one night? I swear on my mother's life I won't touch you. In fact, you can roll up in one of the lighter blankets to ensure I don't. Then we'll put the rest of the blankets on top of both of us."

"I have a better idea, sweetheart." Her voice dripped sugar. "We can all three sleep together. We'll put Piper between us. I think that'll work much better."

"I have to say you have a quick mind," he growled, wrapping it in a smile.

She patted his chest. "After all, dear, we don't want her to freeze, do we?"

"Absolutely not," he whispered. He thought he had a good plan there for a minute, but evidently, she was going to hold him to his word. Which was fine. He really wasn't trying to break his promise. Not at all. Just checking the boundary lines.

"What are you doing over there?" Piper asked. She must've gotten tired of breaking sticks and burning them.

"Well, here's the thing." Jack went to sit on the girl's log. "We didn't count on the nights being this cold, so we didn't bring enough blankets. We're all three going to sleep together in order to stay warm."

"Can we? I'd like that. No bears will get me."

"Nope." He tweaked her nose. "I'll shoot 'em if they try."

"I love you, Daddy Jack." Piper threw her arms around him, surprising him.

Jack hesitated only a split second before pulling her against him. After the beginning days with Piper, he didn't hold back much at all on filling a fatherhood role.

"I love you too, sweet girl," Jack murmured. "I hope you're happy."

"So much my heart is bursting. I wish my mama was here so I could tell her."

"I think she knows." Jack patted Piper's back before letting her go.

Fancy drew her coat tighter and glanced over at them, warmth filling her heart. Piper was so full of love and only wanted to be loved in return. She and Jack would try each day to make sure Piper knew she was cherished.

Her thoughts shifted to Daniel. She was relieved that he seemed to have a loving home. From all appearances, Madeline Bishop worshipped him. Probably her husband too. Fancy's mind would be stretched to the breaking point if she knew Daniel was abused. If that were the case, she'd march right into that house and take her child regardless of the cost. Oh, how her arms ached to hold him again. To nuzzle his neck and kiss his baby cheeks. The yearning was almost more than she could bear.

Later after she and Jack crawled under the covers with Piper between them, Fancy stared up at the stars. She doubted she'd get much sleep for worrying about the men at the mine. Fear of men in general was something she couldn't shake since that terrifying night that had stolen her innocence, ripped from her and tossed away. And now that others might do the same thing again.

What sort of men awaited at the mine? And if Jack couldn't control them... She pushed that thought out of her head. To worry about things before they happened was crazy. Her mother would be sorely disappointed.

Before she knew it morning had come, and Jack raised to look at her. "Were you warm enough, Fancy?"

"I never got cold, and I hate to leave the delicious warmth of these covers."

Piper opened her eyes and stretched. "I had the best sleep."

"Me too." Fancy planted a kiss on the girl's cheek. "Thank you for making my life so full."

"You're welcome. Maybe one day you'll have your baby and won't be so sad."

"I think it'll happen very soon." Jack had propped on an elbow and gave her a stare that appeared to be full of promises. His voice was husky. "I didn't know you'd be so beautiful first thing in the morning with your hair all tousled and sleep still in your eyes, Mrs. Coltrain."

"You didn't tell me you jested so early in the morn," Fancy drawled.

Piper stared back and forth between them. "I'm hungry."

"Me too." Jack threw his covers on top of Fancy and Piper, burying them.

Both squealed in protest and he simply grinned. "Get up you pair of lazybones."

That started the day on a happy note. With all three working, they folded up the blankets and quilts, had breakfast, and were on the road in no time. Jack pushed the horses, appearing anxious to see this mine he'd inherited. As they jostled along under a pale blue sky that looked so near she could touch it with her fingertips, Fancy prayed he wouldn't be disappointed.

She cast a glance at him, noting how rugged he looked with the dark growth along his jaw and the makings of a mustache. It was a comfort to see the gun belt he wore and the heavy Colt on his hip. The top buttons of his gray collarless shirt lay open with a few wisps of dark hair sticking out. He looked like someone who could handle rough miners.

Fancy took advantage of Piper skipping happily a little ahead of the wagon. "Jack, have you ever shot a man?"

He was silent for so long she didn't think he meant to reply.

Finally, he spoke. "Twice. They were cattle rustlers. I wasn't proud that they forced me into making a stand, but I was going to protect our land and our cattle no matter how I had to do it." He met her gaze. "Why?"

"Just thinking…worrying I guess…if you have what it takes up here at the mine. O'Connor said they're a rough bunch."

"And you're wondering if you and Piper will be safe."

"It is on my mind," she confessed, feeling silly for doubting his abilities.

He reached and pulled her to his side. "Darlin', I will shoot anyone who lays a hand on either of you, and I won't be very particular about the severity. All I have to say is they'd best keep away from you if they want to live. Makes no difference to me if they prefer instead to be thrown over the back of a horse."

A cold edge of steel laced his tone, and she couldn't help the shiver that crept up her spine. A threat as deadly as a razor-sharp blade lingered in his voice. "You will be safe. That is my solemn vow."

Right then and there she knew Jack was fully capable to handle anything that came. The tension melted away.

"I pray you don't have to use that gun, but I feel better knowing if you do, it'll be as a last resort." She snuggled into his side and scanned the thick tree line, breathing deep of the heady pine-scented air. "I don't need to know where your money is, only that it's in a safe place."

"It is." He reached under the seat, threw back a piece of burlap, and tapped on a metal strong box. Then he pulled a chain from around his neck with a key on it. "I keep it locked."

"Good. I wasn't trying to pry or anything."

"Stop," he murmured against her temple. "It's as much yours as mine. Repeat that until you believe it."

"It's as much mine as yours." Fancy smiled. "I'm starting to believe, but it'll take a while. I've never owned much in my life. A few dollars here and there that quickly vanished."

"Sounds like me." The lines at the corners of his eyes deepened as he smiled down at her from under the brim of his hat. "Thank you for marrying me. I'll work hard each day not to make you regret it."

"I keep expecting something to change but everything is still the same."

"Yep." After a moment's silence, he went on. "I don't think I'll ever tire of looking at you. Your eyes are extra brown this morning and seem to be peering right into my soul. Makes me a little bit nervous."

"You're a good, decent man, Jack. And you're becoming a good father to Piper. She adores you."

"I hope I don't let the poor kid down."

"Nothing you ever say or do will change her opinion of you."

"Nor of the O'Connors, I fear. I wish…" Jack sighed. "She needs them."

"Yes, she does. They don't know what they're missing."

Piper climbed into the wagon bed and over the seat. Jack shook the reins and the horses picked up the pace. Piper noticed Fancy sitting so close to Jack and gave her a funny look. Then she grinned and settled at Fancy's side like it was the most normal thing in the world.

Maybe it was. Fancy guessed time would tell once the newness wore off.

As a cluster of dismal shacks sorely in need of work came into view, she couldn't help the dread and foreboding that crawled up her back. Trouble lurked on the horizon. Would they be ready?

CHAPTER FIFTEEN

All was quiet as Jack maneuvered the wagon down the path between two rows of hastily constructed shanties built out of whatever the occupants could find. Some perched on the side of hills, barely clinging to the earth. A few women in threadbare dresses and straggly hair emerged from their homes to stare. One waved as they went past.

Fancy waved back. Jack hoped she'd find a few friends here. But he was very conscious of the fact that she hated being so far from her son again and had to tamp down the guilt that kept rising. He shouldn't have brought her, but selfishness made him glad she was at his side. She looked very pretty, so young with her hair pulled back and tied with a pink ribbon. He'd never asked her age but knew she'd seen twenty.

"Oh look, there's a puppy!" Piper cried. "Isn't it cute?"

Jack laughed. "You think all animals are sweeter than stolen honey."

"So do I, Jack Coltrain." Fancy's head swiveled in constant motion trying to take everything in.

They passed a small trading post that was little more than a lean-to. A few horses were tied outside. A man emerged, scratching an armpit and spitting. It was clear that if they'd expected some sort of civilization, they'd come to the wrong place. This was raw, untamed country, and most of the people appeared the same. Scantily clad women strolled from the only two-story structure and called out. Fancy gasped at their boldness. Jack hurried past.

O'Connor said the mine sat north of town, and that's where he headed, praying the miners hadn't made off with everything they could carry.

"This air is so thin, I'm a little dizzy." Fancy leaned against Jack, and he put his arm around her.

"It'll take a day or two, I suspect."

"I have to go," Piper said, holding herself.

"Okay." Jack pulled off the narrow road into the grass and set the brake. Fancy and Piper hurried behind some trees.

When they returned, Jack continued on, soon stopping in front of two buildings that had planks set up for tables. To the left stood the yawning entrance to a mine. A group of men were knotted up, arguing in colorful language.

"I think this is Uncle Anson's place." Jack tried to catch some words but couldn't.

The angry group hadn't even noticed they were there. Jack shouted, but they still ignored him. Finally, he stood in the wagon bed, raised his Colt, and fired twice into the air.

The men stared in angry silence.

"If I'm in the right place and this is Anson Beckett's mine, I'm Jack Coltrain and I'm here to take ownership. Anson was my uncle."

The half dozen miners stalked to the wagon all hollering and waving their fists.

Jack again fired into the air. "I understand that you have gripes and I want to fix the problems. But one at a time." He pointed to an older man who appeared the most levelheaded. "You there. Speak."

"Name's Moss Isaacson an' I reckon I've been here the longest. Anson trusted me to keep these men in line and that's what I tried to do. I respected Anson Beckett and was his foreman." Moss scratched his head and squinted. Like many others he wore a dark heavy shirt, trousers and suspenders. "We haven't been paid nor had anything fit to eat since Cook left. We're mighty unhappy, and the men are ready to ride out."

Jack nodded. "That's why I'm here. I have money to pay you on the spot if you want. But, if you prefer to feed your bellies, my wife first needs to get something cooking. Her name is Fancy, and if I hear one word spoken out of turn, I'll fire you. Do I make myself clear?"

When he heard nothing but grumbling, he raised his voice. "Do I make myself clear?"

Finally, there was a resounding, "Yes!"

"The little lady is my daughter, and you'll show her the same respect."

A young miner in coveralls and work boots stepped forward. "I'll help unload your wagon, boss."

"Thank you. What's your name?" Jack jumped down.

"Theo Baker, sir. The first building there is called the cookshack. The other was where Anson lived. It'll probably be best to separate things out here, if you don't mind me saying so."

"Great suggestion, Theo. Thanks for explaining. I'll do the separating and you fellows can put it in the appropriate places."

While they were talking, several more miners joined them and began the task of hauling things into both buildings. Jack eyed a surly looking fellow standing at the side watching, his arms crossed. Jack's stomach clenched. The stranger wore trouble like an ill-fitting suit. He'd talk to Moss about him and see if he should worry.

Fancy had already climbed from the wagon and stood

with Piper. Jack turned to them. "Let's check things out and get you started."

A horrible smell greeted them inside the cookshack. Food had been left in the pots for what appeared several days, and dirty dishes were piled everywhere. The structure needed a good scrubbing. But on the plus side, it had a good-sized stove and plenty of work room. Scowling and nodding, Fancy walked around inspecting everything.

"This will do. I'll give it a lick and a promise for now," she said. "Tomorrow, I'll give it a good scouring. I wonder where can I get water."

Moss Isaacson had followed them in and spoke. "There's a nice stream out back, ma'am. It's running swift, and cold from the snow melt."

Fancy smiled at him. "Thank you. Mr. Isaacson, isn't it?" She reached to shake his hand.

He took her palm. "That's right. If you need anything at all, ma'am, just ask ol' Moss."

Jack watched how quickly she'd won the disgruntled miner over and had him eating out of her hand. He turned to Piper. "What do you think, gal?"

"It's okay I guess, but where are we gonna sleep?"

"From what Theo said, living quarters are next door. Isn't that right, Isaacson?"

"Correct, boss. What little time Anson slept, he did it there. Gonna be cramped for three."

"We'll manage." It would do nicely for Fancy and Piper. Jack would go elsewhere. He patted Isaacson on the shoulder and turned to the door to see the wagon unloaded save for a few things. Time to get to work. Leaving Fancy and Piper to get a meal together, he went for the strongbox and lifted it out.

A few minutes later, he sat at one of the makeshift tables with the money in front of him and his Colt lying next to it.

"Everyone form a line. Give me your name and what you have coming."

"I have it written down, boss." Moss Isaacson handed him a sheet of paper with names and figures. "Don't want anyone cheating you, so I kept track."

"Excellent. I hope you'll stay on. I need a good foreman."

Moss nodded. "I reckon I'll stay."

With the list making things much easier, the line quickly shrunk in half. Jack felt a menacing shadow fall over his money box and glanced up to see the surly figure he'd noticed earlier. He hadn't had time to ask Moss about him.

"Name?"

"Wade Axel."

The gravelly rasp sent a chill through Jack. Definitely someone to sidestep. He glanced through the list Moss had given him and looked up. "Mr. Axel, I don't see your name here."

Axel's menacing stare pierced Jack as the man leaned closer. "You saying I'm lying?"

The miner's growl rose the hair on Jack's arm. "That's not what I'm saying." He eyed his Colt and yearned to reach for it, but common sense stayed his hand.

Not yet. Wait.

A dangerous tension stretched between them, and Jack didn't break his stare. "I'll pay you a fair price for what you worked but I have no way of knowing the hours. I'll have to—"

"Trouble, Mr. Coltrain?" Isaacson interrupted.

"We're sorting it out," Jack replied, still holding Axel's stare.

"It's my fault, boss. I forgot to add Axel to the list since he's new." Isaacson thrust out a scrap of paper. "Here's his hours."

Jack dropped his gaze to take the scrap. "Thank you, Moss." He counted out the correct sum and laid Axel's pay on the table. "Take your money and either get back to work or ride out. Doesn't make me a hill of beans."

When Axel reached for the money, Jack grabbed his wrist. "If you stay, I'd work on that attitude. I'll have no trouble. Got it?"

The surly miner gave him a curt nod and whirled. Jack watched him grab a pick and stalk into the mine entrance. "Keep an eye on him, Moss. I have a bad feeling in my gut."

"Makes two of us. It's clear he hates authority." With a grunt and a shake of his head, the foreman headed for the mine entrance.

Jack blew out a long breath and quickly put the money back into the strongbox and locked it. He had a feeling in his gut Wade Axel would be a big problem before all was said and done.

He glanced toward the cookshack and prayed for the strength it would require to keep his girls safe. He trusted Axel about as far as he could spit. If anything happened to either Fancy or Piper, he'd never forgive himself.

Tension had filled the cookshack and Fancy didn't know why until she glanced out the window in time to see Jack grab the miner's hand. What was happening? Was the man causing trouble already? They hadn't even been there an hour.

Whatever Jack told the man had worked and he stalked away. But for a long moment, she thought Axel would go for the menacing weapon hanging at his side.

When they'd arrived, the way the man had stood to the side and stared had brought chills racing up her back. He appeared cut from the same worm-eaten cloth as her attacker. Those eyes, that voice were ingrained in her head. Now, here was another to watch out for.

Lord, help her.

"Piper, put down that broom and listen to me." Fancy put a measure of calmness in her voice at least. "Stay close to my side at all times. If you need to use the outhouse, either Jack or I will go with you. Do you understand?"

"Yes, Mama Two. I promise not to wander off."

"Good." Fancy swung to the stove and stirred a thick stew. The smoked venison they'd hauled with them would soon create a mouthwatering meal along with cornbread. It was the easiest and quickest thing she knew to make for a bunch of hungry men.

In between her stirrings, she and Piper began washing the mound of dirty dishes. She wished she could get hold of the former cook. Some of the impossible dirty pots seemed destined for the trash heap. Thank goodness, she'd brought new pots, pans, and dishes since she hadn't known what she'd be walking into.

When everything was ready, she had Jack carry the huge pot of venison stew to one of the makeshift tables. She followed with the plates of cornbread piled high.

Jack set the pot down on the makeshift tables. Fancy took advantage of the bit of privacy while Piper set out plates and eating utensils. "What happened out here when you were paying the miners?"

"Oh, you mean Wade Axel. He took issue with me and thought I was trying to cheat him." Jack gently kissed her temple. "Watch out for him, Fancy."

"Don't worry, I plan to. I already felt uneasy with the way he was staring at me. He reminds me of an oily snake. He has mean eyes."

"That he does. I gave him the choice of leaving or staying. I have a feeling he won't be here long."

"Yes, but what trouble will he make until then? And will he try to shoot you before he goes? Those are what worry me." She was too young to be a widow. They hadn't had a chance to even see if their rushed marriage would work.

The six miners gathered around a raised horse trough. They washed every bit of dirt and grime from their faces and hands before taking a seat under the trees. Wade Axel was the last to finish. He sauntered to an empty bench at one table, his gaze never leaving Fancy. She shivered, kept her head down, and hurried into the cookshack. Inside, she leaned against the closed door, her hands to her face. The man had a way of making her feel dirty.

She stayed inside and ate with Piper until Jack stepped through the door.

"The men have something they want to say." Jack searched her eyes. "Don't let Axel get to you. That's what he wants. Just ignore him and don't look his way."

"I won't." She wished Jack would tell her how to do that.

He looped an arm around her shoulders, and they went out. The men had lined up with Moss Isaacson at the head.

The older miner clutched a cap between his hands. "Ma'am, that was the best meal we've had in a long while. We know you were rushed but it didn't show." He took her hand and bowed over it. "Thanks are not enough to show our gratitude."

Fancy was deeply touched. "You're very welcome. It was my pleasure."

As it came each man's turn, they spoke from their hearts. Oddly though, Wade Axel was not among them, and for that she breathed a sigh of relief. Though later as she thought about it, prickles of fear tiptoed up her back. It was far better to know where he was than where he wasn't. A strange disquiet settled inside her as she readied a bed for her and Piper in Anson Beckett's former residence.

Would Wade Axel be waiting outside their door when they went to the outhouse or for a walk? Would she have to be terrified every second she was here?

A fire crackled in the fireplace, but it added little cheer.

She found Jack packing up all of his uncle's belongings. "Where are you going to sleep? I can make a bed in here for you."

"Don't worry about me." He placed his uncle's shaving mug in a box.

Piper finished smoothing the covers, yawned, and crawled under them.

"I need to know you'll be safe." Fancy couldn't think of anything more frightening than to lose him with men like Wade Axel running around. She yearned to beg him to stay nearby. Not to leave her. But he'd think her weak and helpless, and she had to be strong.

Jack pulled her against his chest. His low voice was raspy. "You've endured so much. I promise I won't let anyone hurt you ever again. You mean too much to me. I'll be right outside."

His soft breath against her cheek took her fear. For now, she was safe and cared for. She leaned back, pulled his face down, and kissed this man who'd married her simply to better her chances at getting her son back.

CHAPTER SIXTEEN

After Jack left, Fancy lay listening to the sounds beyond the small cabin constructed from rough-hewn logs, wondering where he'd gone. She touched her fingertips to her lips, the feel of their kiss lingering.

"Please be safe, Jack," she whispered, then tucked the covers around Piper.

Though she'd feared she couldn't sleep, exhaustion took over, and the next thing she knew, slim fingers of a pink dawn were creeping through the thick window. A log was hissing and popping in the fireplace. She raised her head to look.

Someone had just started a fire. Had to have been Jack. The knowledge that he was seeing to their welfare put a warm glow of happiness. She'd never had anyone except her mother to care for her well-being and it was nice. Really nice.

Her stirring woke Piper. The girl rubbed her eyes.

"Good morning." Fancy kissed her cheek. "Want to help me with breakfast?"

"What are we having?"

"How does venison and flapjacks sound?" The deer meat would run out soon if Jack didn't go hunting. She wondered if there were any chickens around. Mr. Isaacson would be the one to ask.

"Yummy." Piper sent Fancy a worried glance. "Do you think Daddy Jack is all right?"

She wondered the same but had to put on a confident face. "Oh sure, our bear tamer is just fine. Nothing would dare mess with him."

"No, it wouldn't." Piper threw back the covers and reached for her clothes.

Fancy had only removed her dress, so she readied in no time and opened the door to see Jack and Mr. Isaacson sipping coffee at one of the tables. "Morning, gentlemen. I think I must've overslept."

"Not by much." Jack rose and kissed her. "I made a pot of coffee, and Moss and I were discussing a few things. He's going to give me a tour of the mine this morning, then I'll kill some game for fresh meat."

"That will be very welcome." She turned to Moss. "Mr. Isaacson, does anyone have chickens up here?"

"As a matter of fact, I have an indoor coop with a pipe running from my fireplace to keep the brood warm. I furnished the former cook with eggs. I also have a herd of goats that give good milk. I'll bring both this afternoon." He reached down and set some jugs of milk on the table. "I knew you'd need some for breakfast."

"This is wonderful. Thank you so much." Fancy carried the milk into the cookshack as Piper came out next door. The girl hurried over to Jack. She'd worried about where he was sleeping so probably was pestering him about that. Fancy had been curious as well but hadn't wanted to ask in front of Isaacson since he'd think their arrangement strange.

A few minutes later, Piper entered the cookshack and put on an apron.

They were finishing up the flapjacks when she glanced out the window to see Declan O'Connor ride up. She'd forgotten he had a mine located nearby. Given Mrs. O'Connor's seemingly frail constitution, Fancy was shocked to see her sitting next to her husband. Maybe the woman was hardier than she'd appeared.

Piper peered over Fancy's shoulder. "What are you looking at?"

Before she could reply, Piper burst out, "What are they doing here?"

"They own one of these mines. I doubt they'll even spare us a glance." But even as she spoke, the couple climbed from the wagon and approached Jack. Miners were beginning to fill the tables, reminding Fancy she'd best get them fed. "Piper can you carry one platter of flapjacks? I'll take the fried venison since it's heaviest."

The girl backed up, shaking her head. "I ain't going out there."

"I need your help. I can't possibly carry all this myself. Put on a big smile and pretend they're nowhere around. You don't even have to speak to them. Please?"

Piper huffed and picked up a large plate heaped with flapjacks. Fancy grabbed a pan of meat and the coffeepot. They silently set everything down and went back for a platter of food for the remaining table. Fancy politely nodded to Mrs. O'Connor who'd poured coffee for herself and the mister, then headed back to eat with Piper in the cookshack where it was warmer.

The surly Wade Axel arrived late so she was spared from having to face him. None of his fellow miners had much to do with the man either, and that was little surprise.

Jack opened the door and came inside. "I invited the O'Connor's to eat with us. Do you have enough?"

"We have plenty." She glanced at Piper on her way to the stove to put the big skillet back on the fire. "I thought it best to keep Piper company. I hope that didn't seem rude."

"The men didn't mention it."

His smile warmed her and reminded her of their kiss at bedtime. "Jack, thank you for coming in and starting a heavenly fire this morning. Piper and I were grateful."

"I wanted to do it." He glanced at the sullen girl picking at her food. "Your grandparents asked about you."

"Not because they cared. Probably thought it made 'em look better." Piper raised her head. "But it don't, and I don't want them here."

"We will be nice." Jack's quiet voice held no reproach, but was firm and left no room for argument. "As long as they're trying, we will too."

Piper shrugged and went back to staring at her breakfast.

Fancy picked up her empty plate and put it in soapy water. "While you're touring the mine this morning, we'll take a walk if you think it's safe enough. It's such pretty country, and Mr. Isaacson told me the men don't eat the noon meal. They only get breakfast and supper."

"That's right. I think it'll be safe enough with the men working underground. I'll see if Uncle Anson left a weapon in his cabin. I'd feel better if you took it."

Memories of the bear crossed her mind. "All right. If you'll grab the plate of meat, I'll make some hot flapjacks for the O'Connors. Tell them I'll be right out with more coffee."

When she took the hot flapjacks, Fancy was struck by the difference in the couple up here on the mountain. Friendlier somehow. Smiling. Talkative. Very odd. After they'd finished eating, wonder of wonders, Mrs. O'Connor even helped clear the tables before they left.

She took Fancy aside near their wagon and spoke low. "My husband and I talked at length about Piper, and I told him I wasn't going to give up my only grandchild because of his almighty pride. She's all we have, and I want to get to know her. That's why I came up here. I've let him make the rules long enough and flat told him I was my own boss. He's not going to decide things for me anymore."

"I'm glad, ma'am. Your husband has a forceful way about him. Piper's a sweet, sensitive girl and hurting bad."

"My name's Maeve. I'd like it if you'd call me that. Us women have to work things out between us. I'd appreciate it if you'd help smooth Piper's feelings."

"We're going to take a walk later. How far is your house?"

"Less than half a mile around the bend there." Maeve winked. "I'll make some cookies."

"I can't promise anything," Fancy cautioned.

"I know, but if we can just make a start." Maeve's soft green eyes glistened with tears. "I loved my daughter Jenny, and it broke my heart when she left. Declan and she were like kerosene and fire, and it took nothing to ignite the kindling."

Fancy laid a light hand on her arm. "We'll try to make this work with Piper."

"I don't deserve your kindness after the way we treated you but I'm glad you didn't run from us." Declan started toward them, and Maeve climbed into the wagon.

"Thank you for stopping." Fancy waved as they drove off. She'd still gotten little more than a scowl from Declan.

Jack hurried into their cabin and returned with a pistol which she stuck in a pocket. "Thank you. I don't know if I can hit anything, but I feel better having it."

Much later after the dishes were done, the beans for that night's supper simmering, and the cookshack scrubbed, she and Piper set off on foot. Wild plum bushes sported a thick profusion of white flowers, and the strawberry plants were loaded with young green fruit. Everywhere they looked, they found something to ooh and ahh over. Though tempted to venture off, they stuck to the road and kept a sharp eye out for wild animals.

Soon an attractive little cabin sprang up in front of them. Fancy took Piper's hand and headed for the door, but the girl drew back when she spied the O'Connor name above the porch.

"You tricked me!" Piper tugged free. "You meant to come here all along."

Fancy faced the child and spoke gently. "I had a nice conversation with Mrs. O'Connor this morning and she invited us. Please just try. That's all I ask. Mrs. O'Connor wants to get to know you, and regrets the rocky start of your relationship. She truly seems to want to make amends, and I think we should meet her halfway. Don't you? We might become friends."

Piper sighed heavily. "I'll go in, but I don't like it. If she says anything about my mama, I might kick her. And if the mister is here, I'm leaving."

"Fair enough. Let's just see how it goes." Fancy knocked.

Maeve opened the door, wiping her hands on her apron. "Come in. I'm happy you came."

"Yum, I smell something delicious." Fancy gave an appreciative sniff.

"Cookies. I'll bet Miss Piper likes sugar cookies."

"Cinnamon is my favorite." Piper glanced around as though bored.

Fancy hid a laugh. She happened to know Piper loved sugar cookies but refused to give her grandmother an inch.

"Oh really? I made a batch of those too. Come into the kitchen." Maeve led the way.

Ha! Maeve could hold her own in this battle of wits.

The grandmother offered seats at the table then studied Piper. "You look so much like your mother did at your age. You're really a beautiful child."

Piper frowned. "I'm twelve. Old enough to take care of my mama. I cooked, washed clothes, cleaned house, whatever needed doing. Mama said I worked harder than a lot of people."

"I'm sure that's right. Forgive me for calling you a child. You're a capable young woman." Maeve rose to peer into the oven. "I think the cookies are ready."

Curiosity lit Piper's face, until her grandmother turned back around. Then unconcern replaced the interest. Fancy wanted to laugh at the girl's refusal to like her grandmother even a little bit. She had her heart locked up tight and determined not to let anyone inside.

"Those cookies are making my mouth water, Mrs. O'Connor. Can I help?" Fancy offered.

"If you'll get me a hot pad so I can set them on the table."

Spying a thick hot pad, Fancy grabbed it and Maeve lowered the pan. In spite of herself, Piper leaned forward for a better look. The scamp. Maeve caught Fancy's gaze and winked as she reached for some small plates and put three hot cookies on each one.

Maeve placed one plate in front of Piper. "I await your assessment, dear."

The girl took a bite and had to struggle to keep the pure bliss off her face. "Could use a smidgen more of vanilla and baking soda."

"Really?" Fancy thoughtfully chewed a bite. "I think they're just right. So good, Maeve."

"Thank you, dear. But Miss Piper might be right. I'll take her advice next time." The woman emptied the pan and rose to fill it with more cookie dough. "These are the cinnamon," she said as she slipped them into the oven. "We'll see how they turn out."

While they baked, Fancy asked about bears in the vicinity.

"Declan said he's seen more than usual, so please be careful." Maeve bit into a cookie.

"My Daddy Jack ain't afraid of bears," Piper bragged. "He walked right up to one and scared it away. He ain't afraid of nothing."

"When was this?" Maeve asked.

Fancy explained their bear experience. "It beat all I've ever seen. I was scared to death it would kill him."

"Honey, your Daddy Jack is really something." Maeve slipped another cookie onto Piper's plate.

"He's the best daddy in the whole world. And Fancy is my Mama Two."

"Is that right? How lucky you are, Piper." Maeve wore a wistful expression that puzzled Fancy.

Maybe hearing the names Piper had given them made Maeve a little jealous.

They ate cookies and Maeve told Piper some funny and sweet stories of when her mother had been a child. By the time they left, Piper's ruffled feathers were smoothed. She'd loved hearing about her mother and maybe it eased the heartache a little.

Wonder of wonders, Piper even gave her grandmother a quick hug on the porch.

Fancy whispered to Maeve, "I think this was a success. Maybe we'll try it again tomorrow."

Tears filled the elder woman's eyes. "It's so much more than what I'd hoped for. I'm glad I stood up to Declan. He's not going to run my granddaughter off if I have anything to say about it."

Fancy reflected on the situation all the way back to their cabin. Women didn't have to take their domineering husbands. Change could happen but not until they made a stand.

She had no such problem with Jack. What a man she'd gotten. Her lips tingled with the need to be kissed and held in his strong arms. She wondered at the strange yearnings that had taken over her body and were driving her crazy.

CHAPTER SEVENTEEN

Jack's excitement bubbled over that afternoon when he returned with fresh kill—two wild turkeys. "You wouldn't believe what I saw in the mine, Fancy. Rich veins of gold run along the walls. We haven't even begun to scratch the surface."

"That's exciting. But what if someone tries to steal the mine from you? Or worse kills you for it? The chance to get rich often blinds men and proves an irresistible temptation." Fancy shot a glance toward Piper reading a book under a tree and was satisfied the girl couldn't overhear them.

Jack made a slight rumbling sound in his throat like some men did before they spoke. "I won't deny that something could happen because you're too smart to fool. But I have two good men who have my back—Moss and Theo." Jack rubbed a hand across his neck. "Only one man worries me, and Moss and I are positive he's stealing ore."

Fancy inhaled a shocked breath. Though he was trying to hide the fact Wade Axel worried him, he wasn't completely successful. The lines at the corners of his eyes revealed worry. "What are you going to do?"

"Nothing for now. Moss and I are watching. If we can catch Axel, I'll get rid of him."

She gripped his arm. How could he be so calm? "In the meantime, he could kill you."

"He might try." Jack brushed a wisp of loose hair back with a fingertip. "I want to find where he's keeping his stash before I fire him." He kissed her lightly. "What did you and Piper do today?"

"We took a walk." She told him about going to visit Maeve O'Connor. "She's really gotten stronger since standing up to her husband's overbearing ways and swears he's not going to cost her Piper like he did their daughter Jenny. She's evidently had enough, and the change will astound you."

A twinkle filled his eyes. "I told you not to give up on them."

"Yes, you did, oh wise one."

That night, Fancy discovered where Jack was sleeping. He'd made himself a bed in the wagon and pushed it across their door where he could guard them. Guilt rose and she swallowed hard. He was sacrificing his comfort for her and Piper. Yet, there was no talking him out of it, so she spoke her piece and let it go.

A sense of unease overshadowed the following days. Fancy's thoughts were never far from Daniel, and she itched to see her child again. Soon. The bargain she'd struck was almost fulfilled, and a new cook would take her place.

But one week bled into two. Fancy cooked hearty, delicious meals and she and Piper spent more time with Maeve O'Connor. Piper now seemed to enjoy her grandmother's company instead of simply tolerating the woman. A large part of that was due to the fact that Maeve loved telling Piper about things her mother had said and done growing up. Fancy saw Maeve's love. However, Mr. O'Connor still got the silent treatment. If he was around, they usually didn't stay long. Maeve was working on him though and had hopes she'd break through his stubbornness.

"Declan took it real hard when Jenny left. He's walled off his heart and afraid to let Piper in. But I'm not giving up," Maeve had told her at their last visit.

That gave Fancy hope as she worked harder on Piper. Jack was lending his efforts too, and between them all they were determined to bring the two together.

Except for Wade Axel, Fancy had gotten comfortable with the miners. Wade still gave her chills. One morning, Jack rode out to speak to a man he'd heard was an excellent cook and trustworthy. He'd been gone for some time, and she was alone in the cookshack washing breakfast dishes when the door opened.

Without turning, she said, "Jack, you've managed to escape kitchen duty yet again."

"I don't do women's work," came a low snarl.

Fancy whirled and froze. Wade Axel slouched against the door he'd shut. Cold fear arced through her. "What do you want? You're not supposed to be in here."

"Your so-called husband is gone so I thought you might like the company of a real man for a change." His voice, his words were oily and coiled around her. "A woman with the name Fancy has to have a lot of skill at pleasuring a man."

"Get out!" Fancy dried her hands on her apron and looked around for a weapon. "Take another step and I'll scream."

Please God don't let Piper come back from next door where she'd gone for her book.

"I've seen the way you look at men." He took a step closer. "Wiggling those fine hips and giving a throaty laugh."

A large knife rested on a preparation table. If she could get to it....

"You lie," she spat, forcing the words from her dry mouth. "I've never had anything but revulsion for you and men like you. You're filth. Go back under your rock."

Anger darkened his eyes. "I'd planned to save the roughness for later, but we can do that now. Whatever you want, Fancy Pants."

"Leave! That's all I want." She took a deep breath and yelled, "Jack! Jack!"

"He can't hear you," Axel said in a singsong voice.

Her heart pounding, she made a lunge the same time he did and grabbed the knife. Fancy held it tightly in front of her, noting the surprise crossing his face.

"Well, well." He grinned, releasing a chuckle. "Fancy Pants is a wildcat."

"You're about to find out I'm not as easy as you thought." He might overpower her eventually, but she'd fight with every bit of strength she had. "This is my sharpest blade. It'll slice into your belly as smooth as melted butter. Now maybe I will have some fun, but not the kind you have in mind!" She sliced the air in front of her and forced him back several feet.

The door opened and Piper stared, wild-eyed.

"Run, Piper! Run for help! Hurry!"

Axel made a grab for the girl, but Piper was too quick. She ran out screaming.

"You've made a big mistake, Wade Axel." Though Fancy's heart thundered, she forced a measure of calm. Help would come soon. Faith. She just had to fend him off a bit longer.

"Who cares? I have enough gold stashed away to make me a rich man. If you'd have played your cards right, I might've taken you with me." He inched his fingers toward his gun.

"Keep your hands still!" she ordered, terror creeping into her voice. A knife was no match for a gun.

Axel snarled, "I'll leave your broken, battered body for Coltrain to cry over."

She thought she heard a commotion outside the door, and hope soared. She had to keep him talking. "Do men like you ever care about the lives you ruin?"

"Why? Women are here for men's enjoyment. I'm just taking what's intended."

"I feel real sorry for you. You must've broken your poor mother's heart."

"Don't pity me." He made an angry lunge for her. "No one pities me."

The blade caught his arm and drew blood as she leaped aside. He was crazed. She couldn't reason with a madman, but her life depended on trying. "Look, leave right now and I'll forget you ever came in here. Take your gold and ride. Hang around and Jack's going to send you to an early grave."

A scoffing laugh filled the small room. "He doesn't have what it takes to kill a man."

The door suddenly burst open and Jack stood in the sunshine, feet planted, a Colt in his hand. "Want to bet? You're a poor gambler, Wade Axel." Jack flicked his gaze to Fancy before he gave Axel a cold smile. His voice, his eyes were hard as flint. "You should've taken my wife's offer. It's a sight better than mine."

Fancy held her breath. One would win and one would lose. Oh, dear God, don't let it be Jack! To lose him now when she felt love blossoming between them...she couldn't. She had no wish for widowhood. To be alone and having to make her own way with children.

"That so?" The sneer still echoing in the small space, Axel pulled his gun and shot.

Jack dove to the floor, returning fire. His bullet struck Axel's shoulder, and the despicable man went to his knees.

While Axel stared in stunned disbelief, Fancy rushed to Jack. "Are you hit?" He shook his head and got to his feet. *Thank God.* She threw her arms around his neck.

Still on his knees, Axel was raising his gun again when Isaacson burst inside and kicked the weapon out of his hand. Then he grabbed Axel by the collar and hauled him to his feet. "You're not fit for bear bait."

Axel fought to get loose. Jack set Fancy aside and went to help his foreman, hauling off and punching Axel in the stomach. The troublemaker doubled over with a moan.

"We've got his horse saddled, boss, and the gold is secured."

Jack and Isaacson turned away, probably thinking the fight was over. Fancy wasn't so sure Axel had seen the error of his ways. Seizing the opening, Axel pulled a knife from his boot.

"Watch out, Jack!"

In the nick of time, Jack whirled and yanked Axel's hand toward the ceiling. The knife clattered to the plank floor.

Anger slashed deep lines on Jack's face. "Get off this mountain and never come back. We'll spread the word, and no one will hire you. You're done here."

"I'll get him on his horse, boss," Isaacson promised.

Jack had no sooner shoved Wade Axel out the door, than a stranger with a mop of unruly red hair stuck his head inside. "Is it safe to come in?"

"It is." Jack put an arm around Fancy's waist. "Darlin', meet the new cook—Dutch."

For a moment Fancy struggled with so many emotions. She could go home to her son. She bit her trembling lip and reached to shake Dutch's hand. "It's a pleasure. I'm very happy to see you and Jack. I probably wouldn't be here now if you hadn't arrived."

Jack pulled her against him, his eyes surprisingly moist. "You okay? Did he hurt you?"

"No but I fear he would have if you hadn't come. I was lucky. Jack, can we talk?"

Telling the cook to make himself at home for a few minutes, Fancy and Jack went outside. Once away from everyone, she stared up at him. "I'm still shaking. I didn't think I'd survive that." She laid a palm over his heart. "In those moments, everything became crystal clear—how I feel about you and our marriage. The thought of never seeing you again was more than I could bear. And it's not that I was simply scared of making my own way again. It was much more." She wet her lips and took his hand, threading her fingers through his. She took a trembling breath. "Jack Coltrain, I'm falling in love with you."

"I felt that way about you the first time I saw you. I want to make a life far more meaningful than we had at the beginning. My day doesn't start until I glimpse your pretty face. Seeing your smile that lights up your eyes sends joy rippling through me. The accidental brush of our hands fills me with fire. Fancy, you're like a raging fever that doesn't go away." He kissed behind her ear. "If Axel had hurt you in any way, I fear I'd have torn him limb from limb."

"We don't have to worry about that anymore." She kissed the hollow of his throat where his heart pulsed. "Thank you for finding a cook. He has an honest face."

"My feelings exactly." He held her in the circle of his arms. "We'll start for home as soon as you want. Daniel is waiting for his real mama."

Happiness spread through her. "Is tomorrow too soon?" she asked.

"Nope."

A little cry caught their attention, and they turned to see Piper five feet away looking wistful and uncertain. They opened their arms, and the girl ran, snuggling inside their circle.

Family was what you made it, created from loving hearts and an unselfish desire to make the world a better place for one another every single day.

CHAPTER EIGHTEEN

The return trip had taken longer due to heavy rains, and they'd had to hunker down. It was mid-morning when they finally rode into town.

Denver had never looked more beautiful sitting in a valley with the high mountains surrounding it, the snow on the tall peaks spreading light over the city. Fancy loved it because it was where Daniel was.

"Jack, I'm so anxious and excited and scared." She scooted closer to him on the wagon seat as though he could stave off bad news and disappointment. "What if Mr. Kilpatrick met resistance from the Bishops? What if they ran with him, and I'll never see my baby again? What if—"

"Stop." He slipped an arm around her shoulders and kissed her temple. "Don't borrow trouble. Think of the life we'll make for him, and all the happy moments we'll have as a family. You'll get to watch him grow up, find a wife, have babies."

Piper leaned over the seat from the back where she'd been reading. "I'll be a good big sister to Daniel and won't let anyone hurt him."

"I know you will, sweetheart." Fancy patted her arm. The girl had changed so much since they'd first met her on the train. She'd turned into a regular bookworm. Her current choice was *Marnie's Angel* that Miss Susan had lent her.

"Jack, what about your ranch? Aren't you needed there?" Fancy asked.

"I'm giving my part of that to my brother. I've found everything I want here in Colorado." He paused a moment, then gave her a lopsided grin. "I guess if everything goes well this morning, we'll have to start looking for a house." Jack maneuvered the team around some oxen pulling a freight wagon. "We'll go to Miss Susan's first, unload the wagon, and change clothes. Then we'll head over to Townsend Kilpatrick's office. Does that sound all right?"

"It does. I want to look my best." She glanced up at the sky, but she'd been no good at reading it. "Do you have the time?"

He pulled out a silver pocket watch attached to his vest by a silver chain and flipped the lid open. "A little after ten, darlin'."

"That's good." A lot could happen between then and night. She clutched her trembling hands tightly and prayed for a miracle.

Within an hour, she and Jack climbed back into the now empty wagon and headed downtown. Piper had stayed to help Miss Susan.

Jack reined the horses to a stop at the law office and set the brake. She didn't remember getting out until they walked inside.

The attractive young secretary glanced up. "How nice to see you again. Follow me and I'll get Mr. Kilpatrick."

In a matter of minutes, the lawyer entered. "I have good news."

Fancy's heart leaped and she relaxed her grip of Jack's hand. "That's wonderful."

"I spoke with the Bishops and we reached an agreement." Kilpatrick turned to Fancy. "They'll relinquish any claim to Daniel. In exchange, you'll drop all charges against, not only them, but also the midwife Judith Winters. They admit to their part in the scheme and want to make amends."

They would give Daniel back! She couldn't believe her ears. A big lump settled in her throat.

"Did you contact Mrs. Winters?" Fancy asked.

"I did. She's very remorseful and has given up her profession."

As she should. Fancy hoped the woman found some way to atone for what she'd done. She'd truly been distraught when she'd come to Fancy the night of the storm. However, concerning the Bishops, they'd probably still deny her right to Daniel if the lawyer hadn't intervened.

Jack hugged her. "You did it."

"No, Jack. We did it. This wouldn't have happened without you." Fancy inhaled a long breath and turned to the lawyer. "This is far better than I'd hoped, and I thank you so very much. You don't know what it means to get my child back. I've waited a long time for this moment."

"I follow the law, Mrs. Coltrain, and it's clear when it comes to stealing. They stole your child when you were unable to know what was going on." He picked up a small stack of papers from a desk. "Before I have you sign this, I think you have a right to know that Mrs. Bishop has consumption and not long to live."

"I knew she was ill and suspected something like that."

"She believes God is punishing her for what she did." The lawyer straightened the papers in his hand. "I thought you should know that."

"God is not vengeful. That's her guilty conscience. My heart does go out to her though. Giving up Daniel will be very difficult. So, what are the plans? How is this supposed to work?"

"You sign these papers and I'll send someone over to let them know. Unless you have an objection, they'll bring Daniel here tomorrow morning at nine o'clock and turn him over to you."

Her hand flew to her mouth as tears threatened. *Tomorrow.* It was finally happening.

Jack glanced her way and she nodded. His deep voice filled the room. "We'll have to make living arrangements for our growing family, but yes, tomorrow morning will be excellent."

"Then, we'll wrap this up." The lawyer handed her the first of the papers.

Fancy signed everything that Mr. Kilpatrick would file in court then shook his hand. "Thank you for all you've done. I came here filled with so many doubts that I could ever get my son back but you, sir, made it happen. There aren't enough words or money to repay you."

"It was my pleasure. How did things go at the mine?" Kilpatrick asked.

"Except for one bit of trouble, it went great." Jack grinned. "From the looks of things, I'll have a lot more money to put in the bank soon. We've only begun to extract the gold."

Kilpatrick clapped him on the back. "That's great news."

"I want to keep you on retainer as my attorney. We work well together."

"That we do, Coltrain. I'm more than happy to stay on."

The lawyer walked them to the door where they said their goodbyes and left. Outside, Fancy clasped her hands together and murmured a prayer of thanks before she let Jack help her into the wagon.

"I still can't believe this, Jack. It all seems a dream and I'm afraid to wake up."

"Not a dream, darlin'. This time tomorrow, you'll be holding your son."

"No, Jack. Our son. He's yours as well as mine, and you'll be his father."

For a long moment, Jack blinked hard and stared down at his hands. Then he raised his gaze to hers and kissed her in broad daylight. Fancy didn't care who saw. When he let her go to reach for the reins, he chuckled. "I came here a single guy with no thoughts of a family or children, and now I have a wife and two kids. Unbelievable."

"I agree. I'm rather speechless myself with the rapid changes." She leaned against Jack and laid her head on his shoulder, sighing happily. "Let's go check on Reno. Your horse is part of our family too. Then we need to look for a place to live on short notice. We've outgrown the boardinghouse."

"For a fact. The stables it is, then house hunting." He hesitated a moment before grabbing the reins. "I've never asked your intentions before, but would you have anything against living here?"

Fancy placed a palm over his heart. "I like it here just fine." She snuggled against his side. "Wherever you are is where I want to be."

"I'm glad." With that, he pointed the wagon toward the livery.

When they arrived, the large hostler met them at the door. "Your horse has made a remarkable improvement and is ready to leave here anytime."

"That's welcome news." Jack shook his hand. "I won't lie. I couldn't see how he could recover. You've worked a miracle."

"Thank you. I love horses and can't bear to see one injured or sick." The hostler glanced at Fancy and tipped his hat. "Ma'am."

"I agree with my husband. You do amazing work." Fancy glanced around and walked to a stall that held a pretty blue roan. She stroked the mare's face and a heart-shaped white spot on the magnificent animal's head. "You're such a beauty," she crooned.

A few minutes later, Jack came up beside her. "She certainly is." He patted the mare's neck. "Do you want her, Fancy? She's for sale, and we need more than one horse when we go riding."

"Do you mean it, Jack?"

"I want to ride these mountains with you," he said softly. "And I want to teach our children to ride."

"I would love that. Growing up in the city, I never had much chance to ride, so I'll need lessons also. I do love this little mare. Her sweet spirit speaks to me."

"Done." He grinned. "I'm glad you like this one because I already bought her."

She playfully punched his shoulder. "I'm going to have to learn not to look at anything, or you'll spend all your money on me."

"I can't think of anyone I'd rather spend it on," he said quietly, enclosing her in the circle of his arms. "I want to give you everything you had to do without." He brushed a kiss across her lips then released her as footsteps approached.

Jack told the hostler that they'd be back for their mounts as soon as they had a suitable place to put them.

The man walked out with them. "If you're looking to buy outside the city, a cousin of mine has a ranch for sale. He's already moved down south and left me in charge."

Fancy clasped Jack's hand in excitement and before she knew it, they were off to see it.

The property's abundance of trees and water ponds took Fancy's breath. The four-stall barn made it perfect. The two-story, three-bedroom house was livable, but needed some work. She could see them happy here.

Jack inspected it thoroughly then turned to her. "What do you think, Fancy?"

"I like it. I love that large stove in the kitchen, but we have no furniture, not even a bed."

The livery man overheard them. "My cousin left some furniture in the barn, things he has no need of. Even if it doesn't suit you, it'll do until you buy what does."

After some haggling, they bought the property and went to work moving in beds with dressers and chests to match, a large sofa, and a few other things from the barn to the house. The hostler loaded up all that remained and moved it into his place in town. Their next order of business was buying food and all the odds and ends they needed.

By nightfall, the house was almost ready to move into. Fancy was exhausted but filled with the knowledge she'd made the right decision in marrying Jack.

It was very odd how things fell quickly into place when all the pieces fit.

The next morning, gray clouds filled the sky, darkening Fancy's mood. She needed to see the sun, to feel it on her face. Nerves had kept her awake. What if the Bishops escaped with Daniel in the night?

They arrived with Piper at Kilpatrick's law office at the appointed time and shown to a small room where Fancy paced. She was unable to control her nervous energy and moving seemed to help.

Jack rose from where he and Piper were sitting. "Darlin', try not to worry. They'll be here."

"What time is it?"

"Two minutes from the last time you asked." He held her. "Think of the happy home we'll make for our children and the fun we'll have teaching them to ride and care for horses."

"I can't wait, Daddy Jack." Piper got up and came to hug them both. "I'll be a cowgirl."

"Yes, you will." Fancy put an arm around the girl. "A very pretty one at that." Oh, how she loved this child. Then Piper said something that totally shocked her.

"I'm going to spend some time with my grandparents too."

"You are?" Jack lifted his eyebrows.

"I like my grandmother, and I think Grandfather secretly likes me but don't know how to show it." She pursed her lips. "I'll give him another chance. They're old and lonely."

"That's wonderful, Piper." Fancy hugged her. "Sometimes people get off on the wrong foot. Still, it doesn't mean relationships can't be mended."

In the middle of trying to adjust to the new developments, the door opened and Kilpatrick entered. "The Bishops are here. Come with me."

The three of them followed the lawyer into a large room. Fancy's gaze was riveted on the baby in Madeline Bishop's arms. The woman's face was white. Without a word, she carried Daniel to her. Tears rolled down Fancy's cheeks as she held her son's small body close.

"I love you so much, Daniel," she whispered. "I'll never stop loving you, no matter what."

He squirmed and glanced up, staring at her with big blue eyes that seemed a little scared. Then he gave her a slobbery, toothy smile and timidly touched her cheek.

That he wasn't crying was a miracle. It had to mean he felt safe, and that sent her heart soaring.

Across the room, Madeline Bishop sobbed silently on her husband's wide shoulder. He was a handsome man and his kind eyes held tears as well. Fancy understood the hurt they were going to feel, the endless days and lonely nights they'd lie awake. The gaping hole in the couple's lives that would never fill. And that overshadowed her happiness.

Suddenly, she felt the urge to go to them. Clutching Daniel, she approached. "I'm truly sorry. I know the kind of loss you're feeling and how much you yearn for this child. Mrs. Bishop, I'd like us to be friends and for Daniel to see you."

Madeline Bishop lifted her tear-stained face. "You got what you wanted. Don't rub it in."

"That's not what I'm doing." Fancy started to walk away then turned back and spoke softly, "I forgive you. I bear you no ill will."

The woman did a double-take but didn't speak.

Mr. Bishop told Kilpatrick that they needed someone to unload Daniel's belongings from their wagon, then the couple rushed out. Madeline's gulping sobs trailed after them.

Jack gave Fancy and Daniel a hug then followed the Bishops. Daniel started to cry but Piper rushed to him and began making funny faces. Before long he was laughing at her antics.

Kilpatrick stood watching the children play then moved to Fancy's side. "That was a magnanimous gesture on your part, Mrs. Coltrain. Not many would've forgiven such a crime."

"I must in order to live with myself. Hate fosters hate, and I don't want to go through life with that driving me. Besides, I really do feel sorry for them. I know the kind of emptiness they're going to suffer. And they did give my son love and a good home."

"Yes, ma'am." He searched her face. "You're an admirable woman."

In a short time, everything was taken care of and they could leave. Outside, Fancy handed Daniel to Jack. "Meet your father, precious one."

Daniel took to him right off and sat on his lap as they drove to their new home. Every so often he looked around and would start to cry. But Fancy was prepared and always got his mind on a toy or something else. It was going to take time before he'd look at Jack and Fancy as anything but strangers. Plenty of difficulties lay ahead but she had faith they'd get through them as easily as possible. Big Sister would be a huge help.

The moment Jack stopped the wagon in front of their

house, the sun broke through the clouds. It seemed a sign that everything would be all right.

Daniel reached for Jack. "Poppy."

"Come here, son." Jack set him on his shoulders and helped Fancy down. Piper ran ahead, anxious to see where she'd be living.

Fancy watched them with love spilling from her heart. How they'd all found each other seemed a pure miracle. She was going to teach her children that faith, kindness, and respect would take them far in life. How she wished her mother could know.

A bright blue bird suddenly landed on the wagon a few inches away and began to tweet happily. It didn't seem scared of her at all.

Maybe her mother did know.

Jack opened the door, set Daniel beside Piper then strolled back. "Are you all right, darlin'?"

"I'm fine. I was just wondering how in the world I got to be so lucky." She smiled up at him. "Jack Coltrain, you don't know what you got yourself into."

"If it's with you and those kids, bring it on." A teasing glint filled his smoky-gray eyes. "But for right now, I'm carrying my bride over the threshold." He scooped her into his arms and headed for the door where Piper and Daniel stood laughing then Piper whispered in his ear.

Daniel's little voice reached her. "Mama."

With tears clogging her throat, Fancy wound an arm around her new husband's neck. "Jack, I'm ready to be a real wife. I love you so much I don't know what to do with all this joy. You said love would grow, but I never expected this. Not in a million years."

"I did say that, didn't I?" There in a shaft of sunlight spilling from between the clouds, he did a little dance with her in his arms. "Get ready for so much more, darlin'. You've made me the happiest man alive."

This was family—mismatched like a patchwork quilt with a myriad of unusual squares in all shapes and sizes to make a breathtaking masterpiece. Wonderful memories would soon fill their lives. Here, she'd put down roots so deep nothing would pull them out. Fancy released a happy sigh and planted a kiss on Jack's cheek.

She was home.

Books in the 2022 LOVE TRAIN Series

Christiana
Book 1 ~ Pam Crooks ~ April 1

Henley
Book 2 ~ Shanna Hatfield ~ April 15

Melita
Book 3 ~ Margaret Tanner ~ May 1

Lula Mae
Book 4 ~ Charlene Raddon ~ May 15

Samantha
Book 5 ~ Caroline Clemmons ~ June 1

Penelope
Book 6 ~ Heather Blanton ~ June 15

Ivy
Book 7 ~ Kit Morgan ~ July 1

Ainsley
Book 8 ~ Jo-Ann Roberts ~ July 15

Talulla
Book 9 ~ Winnie Griggs ~ August 1

Fancy
Book 10 ~ Linda Broday ~ August 15

ACKNOWLEDGMENTS

I hope you forgive me for taking creative license with the distance from Denver to Cripple Creek. It would've taken them much longer by wagon but for the sake of the story, I shortened it. Also, there were certain details with the train that I didn't get a clear picture of but I did the best I could.

It takes a village to bring a story from creation to publication. I owe Dee Burks so many margaritas it's unreal. She has provided tons of help with not only FANCY, but my others as well. Deepest thanks and much love to Jodi Thomas and her unending encouragement and advice. To Bruce Edwards and Taylor Moore. You guys are always so quick to lend a hand or lift me up. To Pam Crooks, the calm voice of reason when I panicked, thank you for teaching me the ropes in self-publishing and KDP. It was scary. To Charlene Raddon for creating this gorgeous cover and interior design. Thanks to both Pam and Charlene for allowing me to join this exciting Love Train project at the last minute. To the very talented Shanna Hatfield, Margaret Tanner, Caroline Clemmons, Kit Morgan, Heather Blanton, Jo-Ann Roberts, and Winnie Griggs for welcoming me aboard the Union Pacific #1216.

Thanks to my editor, Lyssa Howson and Michele Jones for her formatting skills. My brother Irvin and his wife Connie for reading everything I write. My sister Jean and her husband Gary. Family is so important. My son and two daughters are my life as are the grandkids and great grandson.

Special thanks go to my sister Jan Sikes for always reading and critiquing my work without complaint and the millions of other things you do for me. I can't imagine life without you by my side. You're so amazing.

ABOUT THE AUTHOR

ABOUT LINDA BRODAY

At a young age, **Linda Broday** discovered a love for storytelling, history, and anything pertaining to the Old West. After years of writing romance, it's still tall, rugged cowboys that spark her imagination. A New York Times and USA Today bestselling author, Linda has won many awards, including the prestigious National Readers' Choice Award and the Texas Gold. She resides on the high West Texas plains where she's inspired every day.

TV westerns, books, and movies fed her imagination and regular trips to museums and libraries sealed it. At times she's felt that she once lived during the 1800s because it seems so familiar. Perhaps she did.

She's the mother of three grown children, five grandchildren, and one rambunctious three-year-old great grandson. Linda always looks forward to family get togethers that are noisy affairs filled with laughter. She has six grand dogs that liven up things.

Linda collects rocks, coins, and books as well as surrounds herself with pieces of the past. Give her something old and she's in hog heaven.

A MAN OF LEGEND

Read the First Chapter of
A MAN OF LEGEND
by Linda Broday
Lone Star Legends #3
March 2022
(This is not sweet romance and contains a few love scenes.)

CHAPTER 1

North Texas
Spring 1908

Just because trouble has come visiting doesn't mean you have to offer it a place to sit down. That had always been Crockett Legend's motto, and it had served him well. Until now. Looked like it might be too late at this point for any type of homespun cowboy wisdom. The die had been cast.

Rays of an apricot sky through the idling train's window sent a reminder that his early-morning travel could yield yet more surprises, and it was best to be prepared.

If possible.

He rubbed his face with his hands and glanced around at the people still filling the car. A group of men in rough work clothes were talking about going to the oil fields, hoping to find work in the Texas boom towns that had recently sprung up overnight. In fact, the black gold and talk of getting rich seemed on everyone's minds these days.

A swish of delicate fabric brushing his legs interrupted his thoughts as a woman hesitated, probably scanning the car for a choice of empty seats. Finally, she mumbled something under her breath and took the seat across the narrow aisle from him. A faint scent of sage and wildflowers wafted around him. He glanced up with idle curiosity, and jolts of the familiar rushed through him.

Paisley Mahone.

He sat up straighter. He'd not spoken to her in three years, ever since her father and oldest brother had launched an all-out war with the Legends over a section of land. Joseph Mahone accused Stoker Legend of cheating him out of it. But the truth was, Mahone had lost the land outright in a poker game to Stoker. Now the situation had become a powder keg.

Crockett took in Paisley from beneath the brim of his Stetson. Three years hadn't made a lot of difference. Her hair, still the color of ripe sunflowers, was swept into a low knot on the back of her neck. She stared straight ahead, her light-green eyes glistening. A little plum hat perched on the crown of her head matched the color of her simple dress.

A stir raced along Crockett's body, telling him he'd not spent enough time erasing Paisley from his mind.

Dammit! She was still so beautiful—still so unreachable. Still so forbidden.

A long sigh escaped his lips.

As the iron wheels began to turn and gather speed, leaving Fort Worth, Texas, and the business he'd tended to behind, his mind took him back to a sweltering summer day when they were kids. The ride to the swimming hole to cool off.

One corner of his mouth quirked up. He'd dared Paisley to go in naked with him.

Back then, she'd always been quick to take a dare. Memories piled up. The pointed tips of her breasts tight against his chest. Her wet, silken body sliding over his in the warm water. Sultry kisses of fire. Everything about her was branded in his brain.

Then came the damn feud when she'd chosen her father's side.

In those days, he'd called her Firefly, and the pet name had fit. Now, she'd likely slap him good. As angry as she was, he didn't want to press his luck.

Outside, a horseless carriage raced alongside the train in an apparent attempt to outrun it.

Crockett snorted. Another fool short on brains. Texas had long reached its quota of stupidity.

A bit of the devil got into Crockett. He leaned across the aisle and touched a forefinger to his hat brim. "Morning, Paisley. Nice to see you."

She slowly raised her long lashes, her mouth in a tight line. "Crockett," she hissed.

After the single word, she turned to the window, clearly dismissing him. But he was like a bull charging an interloper, not content to share a pasture or a train ride without more.

"How've you been?" he asked quietly.

Swinging back around, she spat, "I might have no choice but to be on this train with you, but don't expect me to carry on a conversation."

He tried to block out her beautiful features—so close and yet so far. Tried to maintain some semblance of composure. But the little freckle at the corner of her mouth stole his focus. He'd especially loved how that freckle had seemed to wink at him when he kissed her.

She could deny their close friendship, the times they'd spent together, and the secrets they'd shared beneath a moonlit sky, but that damnable freckle made her the same girl she'd always been.

"I'm sorry about—"

"Who? Daddy? My baby brother? Mama?" Her chest heaved, and she shot him a look of contempt. Her voice dripped ice. "If not for your family, they'd all be alive. Before this is over, you Legends will probably send us all to our deaths. Don't pretend we're friends. Or that you care."

The stinging rebuke let him know how far they actually were from friendship. Hell!

However, blaming him for Braxton's death was unreasonable. If her baby brother hadn't run afoul of the law and ended up in Crockett's court, he wouldn't have been sent to prison where a group of inmates beat him to death.

As for her father, Old Man Mahone had died a few days ago of what his short-fused oldest son Farrel claimed was poisoned water. He accused the Legends, vowing to see them pay.

Colleagues had cautioned Crockett about getting involved, but he had a family obligation to figure out if the water had been treated with arsenic and, if so, who'd done it. He knew damned well his family hadn't.

If he could prove it and end this feud…

"Believe it or not, I am sorry," he said softly. "Help me prove we had nothing to do with that."

"You Legends, with more money than God, always twist the facts to make them show what you want. Excuse me." Paisley rose. Clutching her skirt, she hurried down the narrow aisle toward the next car, her spine stiff.

Dammit! How could he fix things if he got no cooperation?

A year and a half ago, upon entering the bar, he'd been appointed judge of the 46th Judicial District in Quanah, Texas. Shortly after, Braxton Mahone stood in his courtroom charged with manslaughter.

The facts were indisputable. Braxton had fought with a man in a saloon, pummeling the guy with his fists until he'd gone down, where he'd struck his head on an iron footrest and died.

Crockett released a weary sigh. He'd been over this a million times.

The resulting sentence had been appropriate. He still stood by his decision, even though it poured kerosene on the fire already started between his grandpa and Paisley's father. The two neighbors had been going at it for years. In the beginning, it had been the land, then fence cutting and missing cattle, each time gradually progressing.

Now they were facing a murder charge. Couldn't get more serious than that. He wasn't about to let the family name get dragged through the mud. Everything they'd worked for, their hard-earned reputation of being fair and honest had been for the good of their neighbors, the community, and Texas.

Paisley's wild accusation that the Legends had caused Caroline Mahone's death was beyond ludicrous. The woman had died on her own property after an accidental fall from a horse.

Now it seemed nothing would settle the dispute—certainly not Joe's death. Far from it.

The door at the end of the car flung open, and a passenger screamed. Crockett glanced up to see a masked gunman clutching Paisley flush against him as a shield. Anger and a healthy dose of fear widened her green eyes, but she appeared calm otherwise.

He sucked in a quick breath, his jaw tightening. Through narrowed eyes, he watched every twitch the gunman made. He had to find an opening.

"Folks, put your money and jewelry in the bag when my compadre comes around. Any trouble, and this pretty little lady will get hurt!" the robber yelled.

Women gasped, stifling screams with their handkerchiefs. One lady fainted. Fabric rustled as men reached into their pockets. Children sobbed, sensing something terrible.

If the piece of horse dung hurt Paisley, there wouldn't be a safe place left in all of Texas.

Crockett eyed the train robber's accomplice weaving toward him with a burlap sack, collecting the passengers' valuables. He noted a slight limp and young, frightened eyes.

This was the robber's son, or he'd eat his hat. Crockett slipped a hand into his boot for the piece of steel he always traveled with and waited.

He turned his attention back to Paisley. Her calm exterior was beginning to crack around the edges. Crockett hoped she'd be ready when he made his move.

Just a few more feet.

But before the kid with the sack made it to him, a potbellied man in a bowler hat jumped to his feet, weapon drawn.

"I ain't giving you one red cent!" Bowler fired directly into the kid, who went down screaming, then swung the gun on the older robber.

Paisley let out a loud cry as Crockett stood, his Colt in hand. "Don't shoot!" he yelled.

Bowler whirled. "Don't tell me what to do. I'm protecting my valuables."

The train robber raised his gun and fired into the ceiling of the passenger car to an abundance of yelling and shrieking. "Put down those weapons or I *will* shoot the lady."

Thankfully, Bowler obliged then stepped over the kid, curled up in pain, and took his seat.

Crockett faced the robber. He moved out into the aisle and held up the Colt. "I'm laying it down. Don't do anything foolish." He met Paisley's eyes and nodded slightly. She nodded back.

Good. At least they'd work together on this one thing.

As he started to place the gun on the floor, she stomped on the robber's foot with her heel and jabbed him with her elbow. The man yelped in pain, releasing her. Paisley leaped aside, giving Crockett a clear target. Taking advantage, Crockett took the shot and sent a bullet slamming into the robber's chest. He slumped to the floor in a pool of blood.

Paisley immediately yanked off her jacket and ran to the

kid, applying pressure to his stomach wound. "Can someone hand me whatever you have? I'll try to save him."

Not wasting a moment, Crockett removed his light coat and put it under the boy's head, then went to check on the older robber. No use. He was dead. Grabbing the robber's arms, he pulled the man to a row of vacant seats, then went to help Paisley.

"Does anyone have a blanket?" he yelled.

"I do," a woman answered, handing him one.

Another passenger offered up a second one.

With murmured thanks, Crockett spread them over the boy. Paisley never glanced up. Her bloodstained hands didn't slow her movements. She stuffed the wound with as much cloth as she could and wrapped torn petticoats around the boy's midsection to hold everything in place. Once, she forced his eyelids open to look. Paisley Mahone oozed confidence and appeared to know what she was doing.

Crockett squatted beside her. "Are you a doctor now?"

"A nurse. For the last year, I've worked with a doctor in Fort Worth." She lifted her anguished gaze, and her chin trembled. "But now I have to go home to bury my father."

"I wish—"

"Apply pressure to his stomach," she said quietly. "Everything else can wait for later."

Crockett nodded and did as requested, moving his fingers over her bloodstained hand.

For the next hour, he worked by her side, watching her, admiring her. Paisley was as dedicated to nursing as he was to the law. Maybe respect and admiration were a place to start rebuilding what they'd lost. But it would take them both, and right now she wasn't giving him the time of day.

Three years without speaking had been rough. One morning, he'd gone to the boarding house where she lived in Fort Worth and waited across the street for her to come out. He'd just needed to see her. He might've gotten the courage to speak, except when she emerged, a gentleman got off the trolley and kissed her cheek. Paisley smiled up at the stranger, and Crockett's heart shattered.

It'd been easier to blame their parting of ways on the feud between their families than to take a hard look at himself. But the cold truth was he hadn't supported her decision to seek something more than marriage. He winced. He'd discounted her desires because she was a woman, and women didn't have careers. What an insufferable ass!

He deserved her scorn, her anger. And more. They'd had something special, and he'd thrown it away like it didn't matter. Like she didn't matter.

"Do you think he'll make it?" Crockett asked.

"I don't know. He's in shock." She put a red-stained hand to her forehead. "If we can get to a doctor, he might."

"The nearest town is Decatur. They should have some kind of hospital." Crockett got to his feet. "I'll go up and speak to the engineer, see if he can get more speed out of this locomotive."

"Thanks." She gave him a grateful smile, a little of the frost seeming to thaw.

In a short time, he came back to report. "The engineer says he has this thing going at top speed, and he's telegraphed the sheriff up ahead." He glanced at the poor kid. "How is he?"

"The blood has slowed some, and he seems to be holding steady." She got to her feet, grabbing hold of the back of a seat to keep from falling as they lurched around a corner. Her face reflected genuine caring. "He's so young, with his whole life ahead of him. Why would he do this?" Her voice broke, and she seemed ready to collapse.

Without thinking or considering the ragged state of their relationship, Crockett tugged her against him. "I got you. Because of you, the kid might have a chance to mend his ways."

The feel of her in his arms was almost more than he could

bear. He closed his eyes to savor that short-lived moment before she pulled away. The coldness had returned. Nothing had changed between them. Suddenly weary, he dropped into the nearest seat.

As they sped along the tracks, she kept working to save the boy—washing his ashen face and moistening his mouth. Crockett tried to anticipate what she needed and offer it before asked, trying to make things smoother for her. At last, they reached the bustling town of Decatur in record time, and they rushed the young man to a ten-bed hospital.

Crockett accompanied Paisley back onto the train, her hand around his elbow. "Please consider what I said. Bury your father and let this feud between our families be done."

"It will never be over until your family returns the Mahone land and pays for my father's and Braxton's deaths."

"Joseph lost that land to Stoker. You know that."

"Do I? Funny, there were no witnesses, and we only have your grandfather's word."

"Are you suggesting Stoker cheated your father out of it?"

Her eyes flashed. "That was his claim—before he conveniently turned up dead."

"If you have proof, I'd love to hear it," he answered quietly.

She blew a strand of hair out of her eyes. "Doesn't your family have enough land, enough money, enough power? Or will you not be happy until you get your hands on all of Texas?"

His temper flared. "I challenge you to back up those accusations with fact. Every bit of land my family bought is aboveboard and legal."

"Are you sure about that?" she ground out through clenched teeth.

"I'll stake my life on it."

"Do you have to be such a Legend? Really? You're not always right."

"I know the values my family stands for and the line they don't cross. Can you say the same of yours?"

Her hand around his arm trembled slightly before she pulled away. The freckle by her mouth wasn't winking this time. Far from it.

Framed by the sunlight shimmering in her golden hair, Paisley took several steps toward the idling train and turned. "Thank you for saving me, Crockett. But don't think this changes anything. Because of your family, I've lost everything." Her chin quivering, she turned. As cool as a winter breeze, she swept up the steps and into the passenger car.

"We'll meet again, Firefly." He wasn't done trying to talk sense into her.

She was hurting and lost, but he'd wait for however long it took for her to regain her footing. Now that he'd seen her again and felt the sparks, he wasn't going to let her go. He'd chip away at the wall surrounding her until it fell.

He had too much to lose to give up on her.

Available wherever books are sold....

CPSIA information can be obtained
at www.ICGtesting.com
Printed in the USA
LVHW012125230822
726653LV00003B/246